THE PROVING OF
MATT STOWE

Ranch hands Matt Stowe and his younger brother Jed are dissatisfied with their tedious, poorly-paid work on the Snake spread. Then the ramrod offers them the chance of earning a little extra cash by travelling to Dodge City and gathering information on the movements of Ned Shanklin, a psychopathic criminal suspected of involvement in cattle rustling. Accepting the job, the Stowe brothers set out for Dodge. But they're riding headlong into far more trouble than they'd bargained for . . .

LEE LEJEUNE

THE PROVING OF MATT STOWE

Complete and Unabridged

LINFORD
Leicester

First published in Great Britain in 2015 by
Robert Hale Limited
London

First Linford Edition
published 2017
by arrangement with
Robert Hale
an imprint of
The Crowood Press
Wiltshire

A catalogue record for this book is available
from the British Library.

ISBN 978–1–4448–3524–3

1

'Matt, I'm getting sick to the teeth with this job,' Joe Stowe said to his older brother Matt.

Matt took the stem of grass he was chewing out of his mouth and spat into the dust. He wasn't in the habit of saying more than was necessary, but spitting made his point clear enough.

'Well then, Matt,' Joe said. 'What are we gonna do about it?'

'Well' — Matt stroked his stubbly jaw — 'what do you suggest?'

Although Matt was the older of the two men by two years, Joe was often the more vocal. 'I think we must go to the ramrod and ask for a raise.'

Matt continued thoughtfully stroking his stubble. 'Won't get you far,' he said after a moment.

'Don't see why not,' Joe complained. 'Here, we're nothin' but wage slaves.

Sure we get our keep and a few dollars to spare. But it don't amount to nothing after we've spent it on — '

'Cigarettes and whiskey and wild wild women,' Matt rejoined with a wry grin.

Joe gave a chuckle in reply. 'Well, that's the way I feel, Matt, and when I feel something I have to do something about it, don't I?'

'You do,' Matt agreed, 'but there's no use in chewing on a broken stone. That way you ruin your teeth and cut your gums to pieces.'

That silenced the younger brother for a while.

In many ways they were alike except that Matt was older and occasionally wiser and Joe talked a lot more, and a good deal of what he said was no more than irritating nonsense. Joe was just twenty years old and Matt was twenty-two. Both men inherited their mother's dark good looks. Their mother Clementina had passed away a couple of years back. Their father, Sam, was a sod-buster who had little time to spare for the two younger boys. He relied on Ryan, his eldest, who worked his guts out on the farm — and without much profit too.

So, after their mother died, the two boys had decided to cut out and go their own way, but so far without much success. Now they were mere waddies working for the Snake spread, so called because of the wriggling snake that was branded on its steers. The Snake spread was owned by a big rancher, name of Calloway. He had come from Ireland way back and made himself rich from supplying beef to towns in the East. Nobody saw much of Calloway these days, though sometimes he rode the range on his big grey, surveying the scene with dark squinty eyes through the blue haze of a fat cigar.

The ramrod Joe had spoken of was Rich Busby, who was as shrewd as an owl and twice as ugly.

The two young brothers had been riding the line, checking the barbed wire and mending the fence where necessary. The work wasn't too hard and it wasn't too easy either; it was just monotonous and boring and Joe riled against it.

The trouble was that, if they cut away, they had very little to offer. Both could read and write to some extent, but Joe had never read a book from cover to cover and he couldn't have spelled a word to save his life. Matt, on the other hand, liked to read and devoured every book he could lay his hands on.

As they rode along together the flaming ball of the sun sank behind the the dark outline of the trees and everything seemed to relax and mellow across the plains.

'What do you suggest we do, Matt?' Joe asked his brother.

Matt looked up thoughtfully. 'Well, brother, I reckon we have a choice.'

'What does that mean?' Joe asked him.

'Well, either we stay on here and hope things might improve. Rich Busby isn't entirely a fool and, like you said, he might see we're ambitious.'

'In which case?'

Matt shrugged. 'In which case we might get promoted in time.'

Joe grunted. 'Like a snowball in hell!' he said. 'What's the alternative?'

Matt paused again. 'The alternative is we can go back to the farm and work our guts out for Pa.'

That caused Joe to pause and think. 'I'm not going back to work for Pa and Ryan. We go back, d'you think pa's gonna treat us like the prodigal sons and kill the fatted calf an' all?'

'You got a point there,' Matt agreed.

'No. I got a better idea.' Joe's voice lifted with enthusiasm.

'What's that, brother?' Matt was not enthusiastic. He was used to his brother's swings of mood.

'I think we should go into Dodge and look for work,' Joe suggested.

The prairie stretched out before them and the silence that followed stretched almost as far.

When they were at their chow in the evening with the other hands, the ramrod, Rich Busby, came and stood over them.

'You boys have a nice day?' he asked in a slightly derogatory tone.

'We done well enough,' Joe replied, giving his brother a sidelong glance.

Busby shrugged. 'When you're through eating I'd like a word with you two boys.'

'Sure,' Matt said. 'We'll be right along.' He gave Joe the elbow to stop him from chipping in.

When the ramrod had moved along Joe turned to Matt. 'What the hell you do that for?' he demanded, referring to the elbow.

Matt was rolling himself a quirly. 'Always listen to what a man says before you make up your mind,' he advised.

Rich Busby was sitting in the shack he called his office when the two brothers came in. He had a lean and hungry look about him and his dark moustaches drooped down on either side of his face as if to emphasize his sour and pessimistic nature. He was around forty years old, a really ancient guy by the brothers' standards.

'Well now, you boys, you got your shooters?' he asked sardonically.

'Our shooters?' Joe asked innocently.

'Yes, your shooters,' the ramrod said with some impatience. 'You know, those things with barrels you use to kill rustlers and coyotes.'

'We got them,' Joe said. 'We always keep them with us. They were presents from way back when we left the farm, but we ain't used them yet.' He was referring to the twin Colt Frontiers their father had given them when they left the farm.

Busby nodded a twisted grin on his face. 'But I guess you could use them if you had to.'

'Oh, we could use them, sir,' Joe boasted. 'I used to practise. I could hit a bottle on a fence post more than a hundred feet away. That's the way it was.'

Matt said nothing. He was wondering just where this conversation was leading.

Busby turned to him. 'You practise too?' he asked.

'Not so much,' Matt replied. He knew he was a better shot than his younger brother, anyway. 'Why do you ask?'

'Well, you know what happened last week?' The ramrod narrowed his eyes.

'We heard something,' Matt replied.

In fact, about twenty head of cattle had been rustled in what they called the south pasture only a week earlier.

'Well, as you can guess, Mr Calloway is none too pleased about that.'

'We sure guessed so,' Matt said with a grin.

Busby ignored the joke. Jokes were not in his department; he liked dealing with the grisly facts.

'What's with Mr Calloway? What does he aim to do about it?' Joe asked. He looked like a newborn wolf poking its head out of the lair for the very first time.

'Well, boys, I got a proposition to make to you.' Busby leaned forward and stared at them. It occurred to Matt that he was trying to mesmerize them with his hooded eyes.

'What's the proposition?' Joe asked with scarcely repressed eagerness.

Matt said nothing; he could see where Busby was heading.

Busby nodded in Matt's direction. 'Mr Calloway and I have discussed the matter and we think we might know who's doing the rustling.'

'That could be useful,' Matt agreed.

Busby shook his head and ignored the intended irony.

'Who would that be?' Joe enquired.

'A guy called Shanklin. I daresay you've heard of him.'

They had certainly heard of Ned Shanklin. Everyone had heard of Shanklin and his bunch. Shanklin was said to be crazy. Not just a little crazy, but downright off his head: a psychopath who enjoyed seeing other people writhing in agony; the kind of guy who would saw your nose off with a Bowie knife and dance while you bled to death.

'What about Shanklin?' Matt looked at the ramrod with suspicion.

Something in his tone seemed to rile Busby. 'What are you complaining about?' he asked sharply. 'You got jobs, don't you?'

Joe drew in his breath and decided to speak, but before he could open his mouth Matt cut in quickly,

'What's the proposition?'

Busby's moustache drooped even more than usual. His eyes narrowed and his eyebrows drew together. There were some rough characters on the ranch but few of them had as much savvy as Matt Stowe. But even Busby knew when it was wise to hold himself in.

'Well,' he replied, 'Mr Calloway wants someone to ride in to Dodge City and have a looksee. They say there are elements there who know a lot about Shanklin. He sometimes even

10

appears in the Crystal saloon himself.'

'That so?' Matt said provocatively.

Busby sat up suddenly and thrust out his mean lips. 'Listen, you want this job or don't you?'

Matt shrugged. 'Depends what Mr Calloway has in mind.'

'And what he intends to pay,' Joe added.

Busby was trying to control his breathing. He looked the two brothers up and down and, perhaps for the first time, realized they were a lot more than fuzz-heads, especially the older brother, Matt.

'As to pay,' the ramrod said, 'that's a matter for negotiation, but I think you'll find Mr Calloway open to reason on that.'

'How long do we stay in Dodge and where do we lodge?' Matt asked pointedly.

These questions seemed to shake Busby even more. He rocked back in his chair and closed his eyes to regain his composure. 'There's places,' he muttered between his teeth.

'There's good places and flea-ridden dumps,' Joe grinned.

'That's two nights,' Matt said. 'And what about the pay negotiations?'

'Shall we say twice what you're getting now?' Busby suggested.

'Is that a month?' Matt asked.

This was getting ridiculous. Busby's moustache almost twisted in fury of their own volition. 'What Mr Calloway is offering is two days extra pay plus a bonus towards the place where you stay.'

'So that's the deal?' Joe said.

'That's the deal,' the ramrod said. 'If you do this job properly, Mr Calloway might look upon you with favour. He might even bump you up to trail boss.'

The two brothers looked at one another in mock astonishment. Then Matt spoke again.

'You mean we ride into Dodge City and snoop around for two days, hoping to get the low-down on Ned Shanklin and his bunch, then ride back to the ranch and make our report to Mr Calloway. Is that what you're saying?'

'For twice the pittance we're getting now?' Joe interjected.

Busby threw up his hands in exasperation. 'That's the deal, take it or leave it.' He gave a snort. 'Think it over and let me know in the morning.'

★　★　★

The two brothers had bunks below the murky windows at the end of the bunkhouse. It was always pretty rowdy in there with the other cowhands, a group of them usually playing poker or faro. Every time a man won at faro a big cheer went up, or sometimes a growl of annoyance from the loser. When it was poker they often accused one another of cheating; occasionally a fistfight would break out.

Joe sometimes joined in the faro, but he almost always lost his stake. Matt, however, preferred to read by candle-light and he read whatever he could lay his hands on, especially stories of ancient battles. Some of the other hands had christened him 'Dude' or 'Pear Brain' but this didn't worry Matt unduly. Not until that night.

He and Joe were squatting on their bunks discussing the day.

'What do you think, Matt?' Joe asked.

'You mean about the ramrod's offer?' Matt said.

'You think we should take it?' Joe said.

Matt folded back the edge of the page and closed the book. Then he looked up. 'I'm still thinking about it,' he replied.

Joe shrugged. 'Get us away for a few days. Like a free vacation in Dodge City.'

'There's nothing free in Dodge,' Matt countered. 'You want to get poorer, go to Dodge.' He grinned quietly to himself.

'"You want to get poorer, go to Dodge". That sounds like a slogan for a holiday poster,' Joe said. 'Maybe you should be in the advertising business.'

Matt nodded. 'Why d'you think he asked about our guns?'

'I guess that's because Dodge City can be dangerous, especially when the waddies get their pay.'

They had both been to Dodge City on cattle runs once or twice but it hadn't appealed to them greatly. Joe had got himself into scrapes there, mostly about women, but Matt was frugal and he wanted to put together a few dollars for some as yet unforeseen eventuality.

'I had a thought about that,' Joe said. 'Why don't we just take the money and run?'

Matt's grin turned to a smile. 'Now, Joe, that wouldn't be strictly ethical, would it?'

'I guess not. It would kind of make us into accomplices of the rustlers and that Nat Shanklin character, wouldn't it?'

But the decision would have to be delayed, because at that moment the substantial form of Sam Shamanzo loomed over them, and quite obviously Sam was drunk.

Sam Shamanzo was the biggest man on the outfit, not especially tall but wide as a house and muscular with it. The other hands mostly kept clear of him in case he lashed out and caught them with his mallet-like fists. If he threw a punch at you he could knock you from here to kingdom come in no time. Unfortunately, he didn't have the intellect to go with it, and, when he was drunk the part of his brain that said 'Stop bugging those poor guys!' went into shut down. In other words, he was a braggart and a bully. And now he was very drunk!

'You guys don't care for poker?' he slurred.

Joe and Matt exchanged glances.

Matt said, 'We're a little busy at the moment.'

'That so?' Shamanzo said. 'Too busy to talk to a man, Pear Brain?'

'We've run out of dollars,' Joe put in.

Shamanzo gave a phlegm-laiden chuckle. 'We're always ready to take an IOU, ain't we, boys?'

The poker players at the end of the room were all studying the Stowes, eager-eyed. They loved to see a quarrel, especially if it led to a ruckus, just as long as it didn't injure their knuckles.

'In fact, I could say we specialize in IOUs. Ain't that so, boys?' Shamanzo jeered.

'That's right,' one of the card players named Lafayette said.

Shamanzo looked down at Matt's book. 'I see you're a reading man, Stowe,' he croaked. 'What's that there book?'

Before Matt could cover the book, Shamanzo had reached out his horny hand and snatched it up. He peered at it closely through squinty eyes. 'What's this about?' he enquired as he swayed to and fro.

'It's called *Ben Hur*,' Matt informed him, 'and it's about galley slaves in Ancient Roman times.'

'Is that so?' Shamanzo peered into the book so closely it looked as if he might wipe his nose on the pages. Then his bleary eyes lit up. 'Did you say 'her'?' he asked.

'That's what it's called, *Ben Hur*,' Matt replied. He was squatting on the edge of his bunk and Shamanzo was swaying above him like the tower of Pisa.

Shamanzo gave his phlegmy chuckle again. 'So you're reading a book about a her. Why not a him, little man? I should have thought you might have preferred hims to hers, a man of your tastes.'

That caused a murmur of laughter from the other end of the bunkhouse.

'Written by Governor Lew Wallace of New Mexico,' Joe put in helpfully.

'That so?' Shamanzo held the book up high so that neither of the brothers could reach it. 'Well, I don't have much time for reading, especially books about hers. Seems to me a waste of God's good time. The hers I like are the calico queens I come across from time to time.'

'Then why don't you just give the book back and enjoy your poker?' Joe suggested.

Still holding the volume out of reach, Shamanzo gave what he thought was a schoolmasterly frown. 'Oh, I don't think I can do that,' he said. He turned towards the poker players. 'What d'you think, boys? Do I give the book back?'

The man called Lafayette stood up. 'No, Sam, you don't give it back. You throw it away. Books are bad medicine for a man of action like Matt Stowe.'

'That's right!' Shamanzo said, flourishing the book above his head. 'Here! Catch!' He flung the book down the bunkhouse towards Lafayette. Lafayette caught it neatly and passed it to another of the card players, who dithered, unsure what to do with it.

Matt stood up, his eyes flaming with anger. 'Give the book back,' he demanded in a level tone.

'*Give the book back!*' Shamanzo

mocked. He reached out with his horny hands and grabbed Matt by his jacket. 'And what happens if I don't?'

'Give the book back, Shamanzo!' a more sympathetic voice said from somewhere at the other end of the bunkhouse.

'Who's telling me what to do?' Shamanzo shouted, shaking Matt to and fro like a puppet. But Matt wasn't a puppet and he had no intention of behaving like a puppet. He suddenly lashed out viciously with his knuckles, right into Shamanzo's enormous gut. Shamanzo grunted and drew back.

'Why you stupid little runt!' he roared. 'I'll knock the living daylights out of you!' Holding Matt's coat with his left hand, he drew back his mallet-like fist and prepared to strike. But that strike never occurred because Joe Stowe had seen what was coming. He had reached behind him and grabbed his Colt Frontier.

As Shamanzo drew back his fist, Joe brought the barrel of the Colt down sharply on the side of Shamanzo's head. As it made contact, there was a pulpy cracking sound. Shamanzo's head jerked sideways and a look of astonishment came into his eyes. The next moment he fell like a poleaxed steer in the space between the bunks.

Matt stared at Joe in astonishment and Joe stared back. Then Joe looked at his Colt Frontier in disbelief as if to say: *Did I do that?*

★   ★   ★

A grave silence descended on the bunkhouse. The next moment, the other hands were crowding round, looking down at the twitching body of Sam Shamanzo.

'My God, you sure done it now!' Layefette exclaimed in dismay.

'Got what he deserved,' one of the other hands said.

'Here, take the damned book!' Someone thrust the book into Matt's hand as though it had been the guilty weapon that had felled Shamanzo.

For a moment the whole bunch of

men were paralysed. They were all looking down at Shamanzo and they saw a thin trail of blood oozing from his temple.

'Dear God!' Lafayette gasped. 'You damned near killed the guy!'

Joe looked at his Colt Frontier in some alarm. 'Had to hit him before he hit my brother,' he explained.

Matt said nothing. He took the Colt from Joe and stowed it back in its holster.

Lafayette was still looking down at Shamanzo, who had stopped twitching.

'Busby ain't gonna like this one little bit,' he muttered.

'We better get him on his bunk,' one of the hands suggested. 'Can't leave him lying here. It ain't dignified.'

The boys all gathered round, and with some difficulty they lifted Shamanzo and heaved him on to his bunk. Then someone draped a blanket over him to keep him warm.

'When he wakes up he's gonna have a hell of a sore head,' Lafayette said pessimistically.

'He's gonna be sore every whichway,' another of the hands said.

Lafayette turned to the brothers. 'You have to decide what to do,' he said. 'You have a choice between cutting out or staying to take the rap. One way or the other Shamanzo is gonna want to pull you boys apart.'

'So you better get a good night's sleep, because you're sure gonna need it, one way or another,' another waddy joked.

In spite of these dire warnings, the brothers slept tolerably well; it had been a hard day and Matt didn't even get to finishing the chapter of *Ben Hur* he had been reading. RIGHNNANCY WRITER THIS!

Some time before sunup they heard Shamanzo groaning and moving about. So he had obviously come to. Matt sat up and got ready for action, but the big man merely fumbled around, wheezing and groaning. Then he made for the door and they heard him, farting and taking a leak outside.

★   ★   ★

Breakfast was usually hearty. Calloway wasn't mean in that respect. If you wanted to get the best from your workers you needed to feed them well. It was usually cornmeal and eggs and occasionally a portion of ham.

Nobody said much that morning, though most of the hands glanced at the brothers from time to time. There was a large gap on the bench where Shamanzo usually perched himself.

When the ramrod appeared he looked along the table and seemed to be counting heads.

'What happened to Shamanzo?' he asked.

'Shamanzo took sick,' someone volunteered.

'Sick from what?' Busby asked suspiciously.

'Sick from a sore head,' Lafayette said.

'Got himself drunk last night,' someone explained.

They all looked down the table towards the two brothers.

24

Joe looked right back. 'He was trying to read a book and he passed out,' he said.

The hands all laughed and Busby gave a sardonic grin under his drooping moustache.

Before the ramrod gave his briefing he said to the brothers, 'Get up to my office. We need to talk.'

The brothers looked at one another and nodded. When they had finished their breakfast they went up to the shack Busby called his office and stood by the door, uncertain whether to enter. Busby kept them waiting a good ten minutes, and when he rode up and dismounted he looked even more disagreeable than usual.

'Come inside,' he said as he swept past them.

They went into the office and stood around like two monkeys, not knowing which tree to climb.

Busby sat behind the ramshackle structure he thought of as a desk. He looked up at Joe and then at Matt.

'I heard what happened last night,' he said. 'We must just hope Shamanzo is not too badly hurt.'

'Self-defence,' Joe piped up. 'He was set to kill my brother.'

Busby grunted. 'Well, Shamanzo won't be riding the range for a day or two and that's a mite inconvenient for Mr Calloway.'

Joe said: 'With a mean temper like that, Shamanzo doesn't deserve to be riding the range at all.'

Busby grunted again and looked at Matt. 'Have you considered Mr Calloway's offer?'

Matt nodded. 'We've thought about it.'

'Then what's your conclusion?' Busby asked sharply.

'Our conclusion is we want to talk to Mr Calloway,' Matt replied.

Busby considered for a moment and shook his head. 'Mr Calloway is a very busy man. I don't think he can find time to talk to you, not today at least.'

'Well, that's the deal. We need to talk

to the boss man.'

Busby twisted his lip. 'What d'you want to talk to Mr Calloway about?'

Matt held his head on one side. 'This and that,' he said. 'Terms and conditions.'

'Terms and conditions,' Joe reiterated.

Busby bit his lip and wondered how to reply, but he didn't have time to say anything more because at that moment Calloway himself rode up on his big grey. He dismounted and strode into the cabin, a fat cigar in his hand. He hadn't lit it yet but he kept it in his hand as a kind of prop.

'Ah, Mr Busby, I see you're talking to these two boys.'

'That's right, Mr Calloway,' Busby said obsequiously.

'So have you put my offer to them?' Calloway asked.

'Yes, sir.' Busby stood behind his pine desk trying to look taller than he was.

'Well then?' Calloway enquired.

'We want to discuss terms,' Joe said brazenly.

A look of intense amusement appeared on Calloway's paunchy face. 'So you want to discuss terms, do you?'

'We do,' Matt replied bluntly.

Calloway glanced at Busby and made a slight movement of the head. 'OK, Mr Busby. You've got work to do. I'll handle this.'

Busby gave the two brothers an enigmatic glance and then took himself off.

When he'd gone, Calloway smiled and seated himself behind the pine desk. 'Why don't you two boys sit down?' he said.

Matt and Joe exchanged glances and Matt nodded. They sat uneasily on two stools facing the pine desk.

Now Calloway lit his fat cigar. He stuck it in his mouth and sucked in deeply. Then he let out an aromatic puff of smoke as a sign of prosperity and authority. A bit like one of those old Roman emperors, Matt thought, though maybe they didn't have cigars.

'Well now, boys,' purred Calloway,

'I'm glad I've got a chance to talk to you. The fact is, I've been keeping an eye on you and I've observed you're something more than the average cowpokes. You have ambition and I can help you in that.' He rolled his fat cigar round his mouth and eyed them through a cloud of smoke.

'What did you have in mind, Mr Calloway?' Matt asked him.

'Well, now, I'm glad you asked that,' Calloway said. 'As you know, there's been a deal of rustling going on. The cattlemen are getting worried and we need to take action.'

'What action have you in mind?' Matt asked, deadpan.

Calloway wasn't fazed. On the contrary, he seemed to be enjoying the conversation. 'The law, such as it is, doesn't seem to be keen to intervene,' he said. 'That's why I want to do a little investigation of my own.'

Matt nodded. 'That seems reasonable, Mr Calloway.'

Calloway gave a self-satisfied smirk.

'That's where you boys come in.'

'Like how?' Joe put in.

'Like I thought you might ride into Dodge City and nose around a mite. See what you can pick up.' He paused to examine the ash at the end of his cigar. 'In fact, we in the Cattlemen's Association know full well who's responsible, but we need to find out where he operates from.'

'I guess you must be talking about Ned Shanklin,' Matt said.

'Yeah.' Calloway pointed his fat cigar at Matt. 'That's the man. And I want you two boys to go full time until you pick up his trail and find out where he's at.'

'Where he's at?' Matt speculated. 'That's a tall order, Mr Calloway.'

'Could be dangerous too,' Joe put in.

'That's why I'm offering you a generous reward,' Calloway said.

For a moment the brothers were silent. Then Matt spoke up again: 'What reward would that be, Mr Calloway?'

Calloway creased his brow and looked

thoughtful. 'Shall we say five hundred dollars when Shanklin is swinging from the nearest tree?'

'What about between now and then?' Matt said. 'A man has to live, you know, Mr Calloway.'

'Well, that's reasonable. Tell you what I'll do. I'll advance you two months' pay and when you come up with the information on Shanklin's outfit another two months' pay plus the five hundred dollars when he hangs.'

Joe opened his mouth a little but said nothing: he knew well enough that, if there was bargaining to do, Matt was his superior by far.

'That sounds reasonable,' Matt said after a moment. 'Except that a thousand dollars would be better.'

Calloway scarcely blinked. He held up his cigar somewhat thoughtfully.

'Well, now,' he said, 'you're a hard bargainer, Mr Stowe.'

'It's a dangerous business, Mr Calloway,' Matt replied.

'Why pick on us?' Joe asked. 'You

need hardened gunmen for this, Mr Calloway.'

Calloway seemed to consult his cigar again. Then he shook his head.

'I've thought about that, Mr Stowe. And you're right, we could bring in a hardened gunfighter, but I don't want you boys to get yourselves shot up in a gunfight. I just want information and I figure you two boys have the brains to do it.'

'Just like the Pinkertons,' Joe said.

'Just like the Pinkertons.' Calloway held up his fat cigar and smiled.

2

Later, well after sunset, the two brothers were squatting together over a campfire somewhere between the Snake outfit and Dodge City. Joe was roasting steaks over the fire. Later he would toss in a generous helping of Mexican strawberries or beans and one or two sweet potatoes he had managed to acquire from the chuck cookie. Joe had always enjoyed cooking and he had struck up a friendship with Jimbo, the old guy who prepared the chuck.

'So, I hear you boys are leaving us,' Jimbo had said.

'Who told you that?' Joe had asked suspiciously.

Calloway had said, 'Don't talk to the crew about this. Just get your gear together and vamoose. No need to shout things from the cabin tops, is there, boys?'

Yet, somehow news of the mission had leaked out and all the crew seemed to know that the brothers were leaving on some secret business for the boss man. Maybe it had something to do with the fight in the bunkhouse when Joe had pistol whipped the bully Shamanzo to save Matt from a beating.

Jimbo had given Joe a toothless grin. 'Tell you something,' he said. 'That Shamanzo is the sort of guy who never forgives. He's well-known for that. Well-known all around the territory. If he bears a grudge he nurses it as close as a she wolf nurses her cub. He's got a sore head too and that won't help, either.' Jimbo guffawed and handed Joe the sweet potatoes.

Now Joe was cooking up the chuck on the campfire and Matt was staring into the flames and thinking. He couldn't have read even if the light had been good enough since the copy of *Ben Hur* that Shamanzo had snatched away from him had disappeared and he hadn't got it back.

I shall never know what happened to that Ben Hurr guy, he thought. *I know he was a great oarsman and he moved from one side of the galley to the other to develop his muscles evenly.*

'You think we're doing the right thing?' Joe asked him when they were eating their chuck.

'You mean going to Dodge?' Matt replied. 'I don't rightly know. I've been thinking about that.'

'Maybe we should cut loose and take the money?' Joe suggested again.

Matt paused. 'I don't know about that, Joe. Calloway obviously thinks he can trust us and he wants to catch up on Shanklin.'

'Either that or he's sending us on some kind of wild-goose chase.'

'Why would he do that?' Matt asked him.

'I was hoping you'd figure that one out,' Joe said. 'After all, you're the brains of the outfit.'

'Maybe we should just sleep on it,' Matt advised. 'Could be things will look different come sunup.'

'I sure hope so.' Joe laid out his bedroll and pulled his blanket over his head. It was none too comfortable, but Joe didn't worry unduly about that, and he was soon snoring away under the night sky.

In fact it was a bright starry night and Matt wasn't such a good sleeper, anyway. When he closed his eyes, thoughts like comets drifted through his head. So he stretched out and gazed up at the stars and let himself drift with them. I wonder what lies beyond those stars and how big they are when you get close to them? Do they go on for ever or is there some kind of a fence up there to corral them in? And if there's a fence, what lies in the darkness beyond?

Deep questions to which he would never find an answer. So he just relaxed and tried to enjoy the maze of glittering stars up there. Now he was riding along with them like some kind of horse-riding spirit. Drifting . . . drifting . . . drifting . . .

★　★　★

Suddenly there was a loud explosion and Matt sat up abruptly. He reached for the Colt Frontier he kept under his saddle.

'Keep your hand away from that gun,' a voice growled. 'Unless you want to get your head blown off.'

Matt stared into the darkness beyond the fire and saw the indistinct form of a man on horseback. The man had a Winchester trained on him.

Now Joe sat up and was staring at the man on the horse.

'What d'you want, Shamanzo?' he said.

'What do you think I want?' Shamanzo snarled. 'I want your heads on those tin plates you just had your chuck from. That's what I want.'

'Well, now, Shamanzo, that's a very big want.' Joe said.

'Not from where I'm set,' Shamanzo growled. 'Now you two skunk heads just keep your hands away from those shooters and stand up real slow with your hands in the air. And don't try any tricks in case my trigger finger kinda slips.'

The brothers exchanged glances and stood with their hands up.

'That's right,' Shamanzo growled. 'Now just do as you're bid and we'll take it one step at a time.'

'What do you aim to do?' Joe asked him.

'What I aim to do is what I'm gonna do,' Shamanzo said. 'You boys insult a man like me you have to pay the price. You understand that?'

The brothers remained silent.

'You hear what I say?' Shamanzo dismounted and took a step closer. He was holding the Winchester across his body, and he had an old Navy cap and ball tucked under his belt.

Matt glanced at his brother again. He knew that Shamanzo was slow, but if they made a move one of them was likely to get killed.

'OK, Shamanzo. So what's the price

you had in mind?' Matt asked. *When you're in a fix, keep talking*, he thought. *That way you're more likely to keep yourself alive.*

'The price is you boys kneel down and say your prayers; that is, if you have any to say.' He motioned with the Winchester. 'No arguments. Just get yourselves down and pray.'

The two brothers glanced at one another again. Matt gave Joe a slight nod and then they both got down on their knees. Joe went down on a stone and said, 'Ouch!'

Shamanzo gave a throaty chuckle. 'Ouch it is,' he said, 'and ouch it's gonna be.' He advanced another step, swinging the Winchester towards them, and they heard the inauspicious sound of Shamanzo levering the weapon.

Then Matt spoke again. 'Listen, Shamanzo,' he said. 'Think about what you're doing. Mr Calloway knows right well where we are and if something unfortunate happens to us he'll want to know why.'

'Well, Mr Calloway can stuff himself,' Shamanzo sneered. 'And the whole Snake outfit can stuff itself too.' The Winchester shook slightly in his hands and Matt knew it was now or never. In a flash he had snatched up his tin plate and hurled it straight at the bully's face.

Shamanzo ducked to one side and fired a round which went harmlessly over their heads. Before he could lever the Winchester again, Joe had leapt over the fire and crashed into Shamanzo's ample belly. The next instant Matt had his Colt Frontier pressed against the man's head.

But Shamanzo wasn't finished yet. He turned away and fell; as he fell the Winchester slipped from his grasp. Matt pressed his boot into Shamanzo's groin. Shamanzo yelled in agony and brought his knees up instinctively to cover himself.

Joe stamped down on Shamanzo and then kicked him as hard as he could in the gut.

Shamanzo had good solid legs. He

kicked back at Joe and sent him sprawling beside the fire. Another inch or two and Joe would have been frying like a prime steak.

Now Matt backed off, still holding the Colt Frontier. But before he could get a bead on Shamanzo, Shamanzo had slithered back on his behind and got his hand on the butt of his Navy Colt, which he jerked free from his belt with surprising dexterity.

'Don't do that!' Matt shouted, but it was too late. The weapon came round in a split second. The Colt Frontier and the Navy flashed and spat almost simultaneously.

Matt staggered and dropped to one knee and Shamanzo fell on his back like a poleaxed bear. He struggled to rise and a look of incredulity appeared in his eyes. He gasped with amazement and a stream of blood poured from his mouth. Then he dropped back, twitched a couple of times, and gave a long deep gasp as the air was expelled from his lungs.

Joe was on his feet instantly. He moved forward and stared down at Shamanzo's gaping, bloodied visage.

'My God!' he said. 'I think we done killed him, brother.'

Matt staggered forward and stared at the corpse. Shamanzo's eyes were fixed open and he seemed to be staring at them with a mixture of shock and incredulity, as if he wanted to say, *How the hell did you do this to me?* But his eyes were lustreless and the brain behind them was stone dead.

'Yes,' Matt conceded, 'he's dead all right.' His voice sounded matter-of-fact, but he was quite numb.

They looked at each other as though they couldn't believe what had happened. Then Joe said, 'You're wounded, Matt. He hit you on the shoulder.'

Matt put his hand to his shoulder and it came away bloody.

Joe moved close to inspect the wound. 'Is it bad?' he said. 'Does it hurt much? There's a deal of blood.' He peered closer.

'Just a graze,' Matt said. 'Might have been a lot worse.'

'I don't think any bones is busted,' Joe said. 'Looks like it just nicked the shoulder muscle.'

'At least I'm still alive.' Matt twisted his mouth in a wry grin. 'More than we can say for Shamanzo.'

They turned and examined the body again. Shamanzo hadn't moved but he looked subtly different as a man does when the spirit goes out of him.

'I never killed a man before,' Joe said, aghast.

'You didn't kill him, I did,' Matt said.

Joe shook his head. 'What are we gonna do?'

'There's nothing we can do,' Matt said. 'He's dead and we're alive. We just got lucky, that's all.'

'Lucky!' Joe marvelled. 'We could have both been lying stiff right here by the fire.'

'You're right about that,' Matt agreed.

'So, what do we do now?' Joe asked.

'Should we say a word of prayer or something?'

Matt shook his head. 'You say a word if it helps you. I don't think it's gonna do much for Shamanzo.'

Joe stared at his brother in dismay. 'You think we should bury the guy? Cover him with rocks or leaves or something?'

'No, I don't think so. Leave him to the coyotes. They'll know what to do with him.'

'Maybe we should drag him off a piece and leave him. I don't want to spend the whole night lying beside a dead man. He might rise up and haunt us.'

Matt shook his head again. 'I don't think so,' he said. 'I think what we do is get our gear together, ride on for an hour and set up another camp.'

'Sure,' Joe agreed. 'That's what we must do.'

★ ★ ★

Come sunup Joe was busy at the fire, making breakfast. As always he had started to snore as soon as he put his head down. Matt, on the other hand, had stayed awake until the first streaks of dawn had started to paint the eastern sky. He didn't believe in ghosts but the picture of Shamanzo holding that Colt cap and ball continued to haunt him. During the night the imagination can play tricks with a man and, though Shamanzo was dead, in Matt's dream he lurched forward like a zombie, toting his gun. You can't kill a man twice but the corpse in the dream kept coming on, refusing to die however many times Matt shot at it.

Another reason why Matt couldn't sleep well was the throbbing pain in his right shoulder. There was no more blood now but the shoulder had stiffened up considerably. Joe had probed around the wound, applied a crude dressing and offered his opinion.

'No bones broken,' he had said encouragingly, 'and no sign of the ball.

It must have nicked the muscle and passed on its way.'

However, that didn't do much to ease the pain and there was the possibility of infection setting in.

Now they were camped by a narrow but fast-flowing creek. As he opened his eyes, Matt could see Joe at work by the fire.

'See you're awake!' Joe chirped like a dawn bird. 'Better get your arse into gear and have some chow. Sooner we get to Dodge the better it will be.'

Matt rolled over and got to his feet. Funny how even the smallest wound can make your body scream at you, he thought, as he disappeared into a small thicket to relieve himself.

'OK, buddy,' Joe piped up when he got back. 'Which way round will it be? Do we have breakfast first or take a looksee at your shoulder?'

Matt chose breakfast and they sat down together by the fire with the tin plates that had helped to kill Shamanzo and save their lives.

'That was a mighty smart move on your part,' Joe said. 'How in hell did you cultivate that skill?'

'I didn't know I had it till I needed it.' Matt laughed. 'Read somewhere how to throw a boomerang and I guess that helped.'

After breakfast Joe peeled off the dressing and took a look at Matt's shoulder wound.

'Looks a mite angry,' Joe said. 'And there's a deal of bruising. I think you should take off your shirt and duck down in the crick. Let the good clean water wash that wound before the bugs get to it.'

In fact they both decided to cleanse themselves in the creek, one at a time so that no unwanted visitors could sneak up on them. Now that Matt was fully awake, the thought of Shamanzo's ghost seemed to fade into the ridiculous.

When he was refreshed he lay on the bank with his holstered gun at his side while Joe frolicked in the creek. That was when Matt heard the whinny of approaching horses.

'We got company,' he called to Joe.

Joe was already climbing out of the creek and gathering his clothes together. 'At least we can give them a clean reception,' he said, laughing.

Matt hadn't bothered to put on his shirt and vest. He had just strapped on his gunbelt. His jeans and his long johns were saturated but that didn't bother him; they would soon dry out in the sun.

Joe scooped up his gunbelt and strapped it on. Just in time.

When they got to their feet they saw six men on horseback looking right down at them. The men were well tooled-up with hardware. One of them, a lean, wild-eyed guy with a rusty beard, looked down at them and grinned.

'So, having a little swim, are we, boys?' He gave a laugh that was something between humour and ridicule. 'Why don't you put on your shirts and come on up and greet us. Must be breakfast time and I could use a good nibble of whatever you have to offer. Ain't that so, boys?'

His companions chuckled in agreement but nobody dismounted.

'Well,' Joe said, 'we ain't got much but you'd be welcome to throw what you got in the pan and I'll be glad to rustle up breakfast for you.' He was buttoning his shirt and pulling on his vest.

The lean, bearded man chuckled and looked back at his buddies. 'Well now, ain't that civilized, boys?'

The other mounted men didn't respond and Matt noticed that they looked none too friendly. Now he too was donning his upper garments.

'I see you got a wound on your shoulder,' the lean man said. 'You happen to get involved in some kind of gunfight?'

'Just a scratch,' Matt said.

'Pity about that,' the lean man said. 'Couldn't be that you killed a man back there, could it?'

'He tried to kill us,' Joe said. 'Why do you ask?'

'No offence, boy.' The lean man turned his horse and backed off a little.

Matt and Joe exchanged glances and Matt raised his eyebrows.

Now the six visitors were tethering their horses close to where Matt and Joe had tethered theirs. Then the visitors crowded to the fire and Joe got ready to start cooking. One of the bunch, a man with bushy sideburns and a dark moustache produced a few strips of venison, which he threw in to the pan.

'This here's Curly, the lean man introduced. 'Least ways we call him Curly since he don't have much hair, and I'm Abe.' He thrust out a horny hand to Matt.'

'Glad to meet you, Abe,' Matt said.

The lean man didn't bother to introduce the other men. Maybe he figured they could speak for themselves.

'The only reason I mention the killing back there is that I happen to know the stiff. Name's Shamanzo, unless I'm a little off track, and that stiff is beginning to stink awful bad even though he's only been dead for a few hours. Full of bad gas, I guess.'

Matt was looking at him unblinkingly. 'Shamanzo a friend of yours?' he asked.

'No friend, just an acquaintance,' Abe said. 'We all know Shamanzo, don't we, boys?'

'Maybe you should say *did* know,' one of the other men said. 'Not much to know now.'

That produced a murmur of grim humour among the bunch.

'Just happened to notice you got Shamanzo's big horse along with you and put two and two together to make five,' Abe said.

'You was always good at math,' the humorist said.

'And you was always good at cracking off your mouth,' Abe retorted.

Another murmur of laughter from the bunch.

'Well, like I said, we come across your old camping place with Shamanzo's corpse lying there, stinking and dead and then we follow a few tracks and find you here with Shamanzo's horse. So, as I say, we drew our own conclusions.' Abe gave what sounded to Matt like a threatening chuckle.

'It don't take a Pinkerton to work that one out,' the humorist added.

Now the five riders lined up by the fire and Joe and Curly started doling out the grub. Joe was almost out of supplies and the visitors had thrown nothing into the pot apart from the few strips of venison, but they were all tucking in to the food with gusto.

'Where are you two boys headed?' Abe enquired.

'General direction of Dodge,' Matt said.

'General direction.' Abe nodded. 'I had marked you down as cowpokes. You don't happen to be with the Snake brand, do you?'

Joe had now doled out the chuck and

he sat down next to the man called Curly, whose whiskers reminded him faintly of a wizard he'd seen in a book of fairy tales when he was a kid. 'We were with the Snake outfit,' he said, 'but we decided to cut loose on our own.'

'I guess you did it just about in time,' Abe said. 'Is that why Shamanzo was tailing you back there? I believe he was with the Snake outfit. He was an awful grudge bearing man.'

'Sure was,' Curly agreed. 'Heard he once wrastled with a bear.'

'Shamanzo always was a bragger,' Abe said.

'Can't even wrastle with a tom cat now.' Curly laughed.

'Are you riding with some outfit yourselves?' Joe asked.

Abe nodded thoughtfully. 'We've ridden with all kinds of outfit this side of the border. That's how we knew Shamanzo. He was a kind of trail bum. I guess you knew that?' He gave Matt an enquiring look.

Matt shrugged and said nothing.

'So you're on your way to the big lights of Dodge City?' Abe said.

'Might be,' Matt responded. 'Haven't made up our minds yet.' He gave his brother a warning look.

'Well, you're right about that,' Abe said. 'A man don't get rich riding for an outfit like the Snake outfit. A man needs to use his brain if he wants to get rich in these parts.'

'You aim to get rich, Abe?' Joe asked him.

Abe regarded him thoughtfully. 'We aim to get richer,' he said. 'We might not end up millionaires but we're doing our best, ain't we, boys?'

The others growled their assent. Abe looked at Matt and Joe with a faint gleam of malice in his eyes.

'Why don't you two boys trail along on with us a while? Dodge is no more than a day's ride and we'll be glad to have your company.'

Joe looked at Matt and saw warning in his eyes. 'Thanks for the offer. We'll be happy to consider it.'

'Well, you have to do that,' Abe said. 'I can tell you boys have a bright future. You got good lively brains between those ears of yours.'

'You sure do,' the humorist added. 'I can smell your thoughts churning over from here.'

The other men laughed, not heartily, but in a tone that roused Matt's suspicions. He was becoming certain of one thing: this band of riders were intent on some kind of criminal activity in which he and his brother would not want to be involved.

'I think we'll just bide here for a while,' he said. 'We've got plans to talk over.'

'Of course you do,' Abe agreed. 'And that makes good sense. But, before we say thanks a lot for that good breakfast, there's one other thing I'd like to say . . . '

The next moment Matt was looking down the barrel of a Remington shooter. 'OK, boys,' Abe said to the bunch. 'Take a looksee at what they've got. Small pickings, I guess. A few dollars, maybe. Two fine horses. Not much else.'

The humorist had a gun trained on Joe and he was laughing.

'Sorry to do this to you, sonny, but in future never talk to strange men. Remember no man is quite what he seems to be.'

He and Curly held their guns on the brothers while Abe and the rest searched their belongings and went through their saddle-bags. Then they gathered together all the brothers' food supplies and mounted their horses. Abe knew his business. He had taken the two Colt Frontiers and the gunbelts.

'Tell you what,' he said to the brothers. 'Since you were so welcoming I don't aim to be mean. You kids need to have a chance in the world. On account of you welcoming us and the fact that you rid the world of that bully Shamanzo, I'm going to leave you your guns with enough shells to protect yourselves, and Shamanzo's horse. He's bit on the scraggy side but he'll carry the two of you with ease.'

'What about our own horses?' Joe asked him.

'Well,' Abe said, 'I'm sorry to inconvenience you, but they come with us. Right now our need is greater than yours.'

The six men mounted up.

'*Adios, amigos!*' Abe waved to the two brothers. The humorist laughed in a high-pitched voice, and they rode away.

'What do we do now?' Joe asked in dismay.

Matt shrugged and considered matters. He had a strong sense of defeat and not for the first time. It seemed that since they left the Snake spread there had been some kind of jinx on them.

'First we check and see what they left us,' he said.

'Well, at least we've got our loaded guns,' Joe said with a grin.

'And the horse,' Matt added. 'That

means we don't have to walk.'

'No chuck,' Joe complained. 'They cleaned us right out of food — and dollars, too.'

Matt was busy checking his Colt Frontier. There were six rounds in the revolving chamber. Matt was no gunfighter but he sure would draw on that Abe character if he met him again.

'The way I figure it,' Joe said, 'either we go on or we go back.'

Matt grimaced. 'Well, brother, we can't go back, that's for sure. Can you imagine what would happen if we appeared before Calloway riding on Shamanzo's camp staller and with no dollars in our pockets. Not to mention the hands. You'd hear them laughing from here to hell's end.'

'You got a point there,' Joe agreed. 'But we'd look almost as foolish riding into Dodge on one horse. Not to mention the fact that someone might recognize Shamanzo's horse and put two and two together.'

'That may be so,' Matt said. 'But I

don't think we have any other option. Anyway, Dodge is closer and I think we have to go on. And . . . ' He paused.

'And what?' asked Joe.

'And, who knows, we might catch up on those skookums on the way.'

'You got a point there,' Joe said. NAH.CRAP.

3

At that time Dodge City was one of the most lawless towns not only in Kansas but in the whole of Western America. It was full of gamblers, gunfighters, hard drinkers, and girls of the line. The infamous calico queen Timberline had plied her trade there until drugs, booze, and debauchery had ruined her looks and killed her off. And well-known gunfighters like Wyatt Earp and Bat Masterson had combined forces to keep order under the aegis of the Dodge City Peace Commission. They had put up a notice on the road into town asking those who arrived to 'refrain from carrying firearms within the city limits'. Nobody had much regard for the law in and around Dodge City and there had been many gunfights within those city limits, many of them with fatal consequences.

When the two brothers rode in on Shamanzo's horse it was late afternoon and things were starting to hot up in the gaming houses and saloons. Two young *hombres* riding on one horse invited ridicule and men and women were seen smirking and pointing from every doorway. But Matt and Joe paid no heed: they were just glad to have reached their destination.

When they arrived outside the famous Long Branch saloon, they dismounted and considered their position.

'What do we do now?' Joe asked his brother.

'We go inside and take a drink and maybe a little grub. My belly is flapping against my ribs.'

They hadn't eaten since breakfast but by good fortune Matt had managed to preserve a few dollars which he had sewn up in his pants and had managed to conceal when Abe and his bunch stole their belongings, including their two good horses.

They hitched Shamanzo's horse to

the hitching-rail and ventured into the interior. The place was seething and noisy. Someone was playing a honky-tonk piano and couples were shuffling about in what they thought was a dance. Beyond the gyrating dancers there were several tables accommodating poker players, most of them peering at one another poker-faced from under big hats that half-covered their eyes.

'Why don't we get into a game and rake in a few more dollars?' Joe suggested with a laugh.

'More likely lose your shirt.' Matt grinned. He knew only too well that Joe had a hankering to gamble dollars on a game of chance.

Joe just nodded but his eyes were shining with the excitement of the establishment. *This is the life!* he was thinking, but before he could give expression to his enthusiasm they were confronted by a blowsy woman all tricked out with frills and gaudy furbelows.

'You boys just ridden into town?' she asked, looking them up and down and wondering whether they had any money she could squeeze out of them.

'We just got in,' Joe said.

'Thought there might be a table where we could perch ourselves and take a drink,' Matt said.

'You wouldn't be looking for a place to stay, would you?' she enquired with an arch look.

Joe opened his mouth to speak, but, before he could utter a word, Matt said: 'We'd just like a table, miss. That's all we want for the moment.'

'Why don't you boys sit down here?' a voice asked from close by. They looked round and saw a man of about sixty or sixty-five, or could have been seventy, sitting at a table on his own with two empty chairs. He had a greyish, well-lined face and a large walrus-type moustache. But what Matt noticed chiefly was the lively twinkle in his old eyes. *Just like the* Ancient Mariner *in the poem I once read*, Matt thought.

'Well, thank you, sir.' He sat down across the table from the old man.

Joe was still staring open-mouthed at the buxom woman with the frills and furbelows as she glanced back and gave him the glad-eye look.

'Why don't you sit down, country boy?' the old man said to him, 'before your mouth opens so wide you gulp the whole saloon up?'

Joe shook his head and sat down beside his brother.

'So you two boys just got in?' the old man asked.

'This very minute,' Joe replied with the eager look still bright in his eyes.

'Well, you got to be careful,' the old man said. 'This town is always on the lookout for young suckers like you.' He gave a laugh like the yap of a big friendly dog. 'No offence, boys. I'm Stephen Inkpen, late United States marshal.' He stretched out a large paw and shook each of them by the hand. 'Late in the sense I'm not dead but retired.' He nodded. 'Caught a whole bunch of villains in my time. Even had to shoot a few. You might ask me why

I'm sitting here in this den of iniquity. The reason is I like people-watching. This old world might be nothing but a heap of horse-shit, but I still find its inhabitants fascinating. You boys ever indulge in people-watching?'

'Yes sir,' Joe replied. 'I always watch people when I get the chance.'

'So I've noticed.' The ex-marshal's eyes twinkled. 'By the way, have yourselves a shot of whiskey. There's water too, if you want it.' He pushed a bottle of whiskey towards them. 'Help yourselves, boys.'

'Thank you kindly, sir.' Joe poured a finger of whiskey into each glass. He tilted his own glass at the ex-marshal.

Matt took up his glass and examined the contents. It looked pale but strong.

'Good whiskey,' he said after taking a sip.

'Some places they water it down and mix in other stuff. You ever come across Prickly Ash bitters?'

'No, sir,' Joe said. 'Can't say I ever have.'

'Well, my advice is don't touch it. It's brewed from some godawful shrub called Prickly Ash and it's almost as deadly as the hooch they dish out to the Indians. Makes a man fighting mad, too.'

Matt said, 'Thanks for the warning, Marshal. We'll bear that in mind.'

'Another thing' — Steve Inkpen raised his glass — 'don't eat here unless you have to. The food is nothing but a heap of crap.'

'Thanks again.' Matt clinked glasses with him. 'But I'm afraid it's a little late for that.' They had already ordered their steaks and a man in a black tail coat and trousers was carrying them to the table. He placed the plates before them with a flourish as though offering them steaming ambrosia.

'Will there anything else, gentlemen?'

'I think that will be all,' the ex-marshal replied on their behalf.

'Perhaps you'd be so kind as to pay at the table?' the waiter said.

Matt and Joe exchanged glances and

Matt knew they didn't have enough dollars to pay the bill. Steve Inkpen was studying them closely with his eagle eyes.

'Tell you what, boys,' he said. 'Have this round on me.'

Matt and Joe looked at him in astonishment. *What's the catch?* Matt was wondering.

Steve Inkpen shook his head. 'You two boys were read any fairy tales?' he asked.

'Read one once,' Joe said. 'Something about two kids lost deep in a wood.'

The ex-marshal held up a finger. 'The very one I had in mind. When I saw you two boys come in through those doors, you reminded me of those kids lost in the dark wood and the witch who fattened them up for her Christmas dinner.'

'Why was that, sir?' Joe asked innocently.

'That's because there are plenty of witches and wizards in this town waiting to gobble up boys like you.' He turned his attention to Matt. 'I guess you might wonder if I'm one of those very wizards myself?' he said.

Matt gave a slight nod. 'It had crossed my mind.'

'And you are saying to yourself, 'Why would this old guy pick on us as a worthy cause?' Is that right?'

'That occurred to me too,' Matt said.

Steve Inkpen sat back in his chair and took out a cheroot which he tapped on the table top thoughtfully.

'Well, it's like this,' he said. 'I knew as soon as you came in here you hadn't got a bean between you and unless someone provided a little help you'd soon be gobbled right up or kicked out in the street. So I thought I'd do my good deed for the day.'

'How come?' Joe asked, wide-eyed.

The ex-marshal lit his cheroot from a candle flame on the table, then he peered at them through two shrewd eyes.

'My guess is you've been in some sort of trouble recently and you haven't got two beans to rub together. Am I right?'

The brothers exchanged glances, in Joe's case one of astonishment, in Matt's case one of scepticism.

'You must be a mind-reader, Marshal,' Joe said.

Inkpen shrugged. 'When you've been a law enforcer as long as I have, you learn to observe and draw conclusions.'

Then Joe started telling him how they had been waylaid and robbed at gunpoint by Abe and his gang. He didn't mention the Snake outfit or the fact that Calloway had paid them to investigate the whereabouts of a certain cattle rustler named Ned Shanklin.

Steve Inkpen continued to smoke his cheroot, nodding occasionally.

'You mentioned Abe,' he said.

'You heard of him?' Matt asked.

Inkpen chuckled to himself. 'I sure have,' he said. 'He's one of those wizards and witches I spoke of. I had the pleasure of putting him behind bars some time back. If we're talking about the same person, it will be Abe Benjamin. You say he stole your horses and your money but he left you with your shooters and just enough shells to keep yourself alive. That sounds like Abe. He'd steal the milk from a baby's mouth.'

Matt and Joe didn't look at one another. They both felt like damned fools. Inkpen took the cheroot out of his mouth and crushed it into the candle holder.

'Well now, boys, I'd like to put a proposition to you. I have a small spread no more than a mile out of town. Just a few chickens and cows. It doesn't amount to much but it keeps us more than busy. We could use a little help . . . just for a couple of days. So why don't you come to the spread and accept our hospitality. No strings. We'd be pleased to welcome you.'

Now the brothers did exchange glances and, after a moment, Matt nodded.

'Good,' the ex-marshal said with a smile. 'Then we should leave right now. How about that?' He looked down at their half empty plates and wrinkled his nose. 'Don't bother to eat any more of that crap in case it kills you off before you get to the spread.'

He lumbered up from the table and made for the door. Considering he was almost as old as Methuselah, he was surprisingly nimble. As the brothers followed him they noticed that inquisitive eyes gazed at them as they passed. Apparently, Marshal Stephen Inkpen was a well-known character in the saloon.

'Got my buggy right here,' he announced from under the shade of the *ramada*. 'Is that apology for a horse yours?' He nodded towards Shamanzo's horse.

The brothers didn't explain. They just took the horse to the drinking-trough and let it drink. Then they tethered it to Inkpen's buggy, got on board and rode out of town.

* * *

As the ex-marshal had said, his spread was little more than a mile out of town. Close enough to get supplies but not close enough to be unduly disturbed by the noise of an unruly city. Inkpen had said 'we' and 'us' when he referred to the welcome they would receive and Matt wondered just who the other partners in the enterprise might be. When they drew close to Inkpen's spread or ranch they were in for a surprise. For one thing, it wasn't quite as modest as they had expected. Though the ranch house wasn't large, it appeared from what they could see in the gloaming to be quite well set up.

As they rode in under the buffalo skull above the drive in, the old man gave a yell. Three figures appeared at the door of the ranch house, one of them holding up a lantern.

'Is that you, Pa?' a voice called out.

'Yes, it's me for sure!' the old man crowed. 'Now, why don't you two boys climb down and go right inside?' he said to the brothers.

Matt and Joe got down from the buggy as a young woman came forward to unhitch the horses.

'And give that poor beast a feed,'

Inkpen said, referring to the Shamanzo horse.

'Yes, Pa,' the young woman replied.

'Come right in,' the woman in the doorway said. She raised the Remington double barrel shotgun she carried so that it pointed to the sky.

The brothers walked into the ranch house and the first thing Matt noticed was that the interior was tidy and clean as a new pin.

The two brothers were holding their hats in their hands and staring around as though they had just entered some kind of fairy-tale palace. The woman with the shotgun rested her grey eyes on them and seemed to consider.

'You meet him in the saloon?' she asked in a voice that was cracked like that of the witch in the fairy tale.

'Yes, ma'am.' Joe gave a kind of bow.

The next moment Steve Inkpen came into the room. He was grinning amiably under his big walrus moustache.

'Well, this is the castle,' he said, 'And this here is my good woman, May.'

The two brothers shook hands with the good woman. Matt noticed that her grip was as strong as that of a man. She was clearly a hard-working woman of no mean account.

'And this here is my youngest daughter, Bethany.'

They turned towards Bethany and saw that she was a complete contrast to her mother. She had a smooth complexion, ripe-apple cheeks and the twinkling eyes of her pa. When they shook hands with her she gave them a slight curtsy.

Then the older daughter came into the cabin and Matt saw that she favoured her mother more. She was somewhat leaner than Bethany but she too had her father's twinkling eyes.

'And this is Annabelle,' the old man said.

'Just call me Bell,' she said in a voice not dissimilar to her mother's.

'I brought these two wandering souls in from the storm,' Steve Inkpen explained.

The brothers just stood there smiling

uneasily and looking somewhat sheepish.

'Well, I guess you can use some dinner,' May Inkpen said. 'Why don't you just set yourselves down and share our meal with us?'

Bethany, the younger daughter who, Matt figured, was about eighteen, gestured towards the well-scrubbed pine table.

'Well, thank you,' Joe said eagerly. 'We did eat something earlier in the Long Branch saloon.'

'That was just horse manure,' Inkpen said. 'They couldn't eat but half of it without being sick to the stomach.'

'I think we could do better than that,' May Inkpen said. 'You look like you need feeding up.'

The brothers sat down opposite the sisters. Joe was opposite Bell, the older girl, and Matt found himself across from Beth, the younger one.

May produced a huge pot of roast chicken with vegetables and started dishing them out on china plates, while

Steve Inkpen beamed down the length of the table at her.

'Cooks like the Angel Gabriel,' he told the boys. 'Not that angels do a lot of cooking in Heaven. I don't suppose they eat much up there, do they? Don't need common or garden food to nourish their spiritual bodies.' He lowered his voice. 'Shall we say a word of prayer before we pitch in?'

At the end of the meal, Steve Inkpen belched loudly and got up from the table. 'Now, you boys follow me and I'll show you to your quarters.'

Matt and Joe thanked May for the wonderful dinner and gave the sisters a smile and a nod. Then they followed Steve Inkpen's swinging lantern out to the barn.

'Sorry you have to rest in the barn,' he said, 'but we don't have room in the house. Some time I might build on another wing but right now this is all we have.'

Matt looked up at the stars and saw they were twinkling away just like they were talking together. Steve Inkpen showed them into the barn and held the lantern up.

'Well, here it is, boys. Just snuggle down in the hay and rest your bones till sunup.'

'What happens then?' Joe asked.

The old man hooted. 'We'll think about that come morning. Live for the moment. That's my philosophy.' The next second he was bobbing away with the lantern towards the ranch house.

Matt and Joe took off their boots and made themselves comfortable amidst the hay.

'You know what,' Joe said. 'I think we got lucky here, brother.'

'It seems so,' Matt agreed. As usual he was a little more wary; he wondered whether the old man was generous or just plain loco.

'Did you see the way those two beautiful girls looked at us?' Joe said.

'The way that Bethany looked at you I did notice,' Matt said. 'But I'm wondering why the old man took us in like two beggars at the feast.'

Joe chuckled. 'We'll soon find out in the morning.'

Matt was thinking of the two kids lost in the wild woods as he started drifting off to sleep.

* * *

He hadn't slept for more than an hour when he was awakened by the light from a flaming torch shining on his face. What the hell! he thought as he sat up and reached for his gun. Then he heard voices.

'Burn the whole place down!' someone whispered harshly.

'Burn them out of house and home!' another voice agreed. 'That crazy marshal deserves what he gets!'

In an instant Matt was on his feet with his gun in his hand. He shook Joe violently with his left hand.

'What the hell!' Joe said.

'Get your gun and follow me.' Matt darted to one side of the door and the man with the torch raised it above his head and stared full into his face.

'My gawd!' he said. 'We got men in here.'

Matt fired a round from the Colt Frontier. The man drew back quickly and flung the flaming torch in his direction.

'Kick it out!' Matt shouted. Joe ran forward and gave the flaming torch a hefty kick which sent it spinning towards the retreating figures.

The two brothers ran forward, then dropped down into a kneeling position.

'Remember we don't have extra shells,' Matt warned his brother.

Now in the moonlight they could distinguish men on horseback, maybe as many as half a dozen. He saw the flash of their guns as they fired towards them. But in this light, bright as it was, you couldn't hope to bring down a bat.

'Hold your fire!' he called to his brother. But Joe trotted forward and knelt again.

The next instant they heard the blast

of a shotgun from the direction of the ranch house. Old Steve Inkpen came lurching towards them carrying a Winchester.

'Did you boys see them?' he shouted.

'We saw them right enough,' Matt said. 'They wanted to burn the barn down.'

The old man stood looking around into the night. 'Well, I'll be damned!' he said. 'Good job you boys were around or we might have have been fried to cinders in our own beds.'

'I'm afraid we brought you bad luck,' Matt said.

'No, you brought good luck!' the old man contradicted. 'It seems you boys are guardian angels.'

'What d'you think we should do?' Joe asked him. 'Should we go after them?'

'Not likely, boys. They might be any-where. We just sit tight and wait until sunup. Then we decide what's best to do.'

Nevertheless, they decided to take turns keeping watch in case the raiders returned.

★   ★   ★

In the light of day things always look less threatening, and they all sat round the pine table enjoying a hearty breakfast. May Inkpen and the two girls obviously thought the two brothers were heroes.

Matt and Joe tucked into their lavish breakfasts with hearty appetites.

Steve Inkpen went to the door and looked out across the prairie. 'Ghosts from the past,' he said. 'When you've been in the law business they always come back to haunt you sooner or later.' When he turned from the door he had a grim smile on his face. 'That's what life is about,' he added. 'Everything you do comes back sooner or later and you have to expect that.'

'Do you have a thought about who it might have been last night?' his wife asked.

Steve drew his brows together in a frown. 'Could be any one of a number of villains,' he said.

Matt was just devouring a slice of delicious ham. He rested his fork on the edge of his plate and said. 'I think I know who they were.'

Joe looked at him and grinned. 'So do I too,' he added.

The three women were looking at Matt in amazement.

Steve Inkpen nodded. 'Are you going to enlighten us, young man?'

Matt paused for a moment. 'Well, I recognized their voices. Unless I'm very much mistaken they were that Abe and his bunch, the men who caught up with us at the creek and stole our money and our horses.'

Steve's eyes were gleaming with intelligence. 'Abe Benjamin,' he said. 'That would figure.'

'Wasn't he one of the villains you put behind bars some time back?' May Inkpen asked him.

Inken nodded. 'He was indeed.'

'Maybe they followed us here,' Joe speculated.

Matt shook his head decisively. 'Not

at all. What would be the point of that?'

'No point at all. Mere coincidence,' the marshal said. He turned to Matt. 'What is more to the point is, what do you boys intend to do about it?'

Matt narrowed his eyes. 'If we knew where those skookums were headed we could follow them and get our horses back.'

Steve Inkpen jerked his head to one side. 'Maybe we should go and have a looksee. We might pick their trail and see which way they might be headed.'

May looked at her husband in dismay. 'Now, Stephen Inkpen, you're far too old to go trailing around the open prairie, tracking down bad men.'

'Besides which we need a man here to keep watch,' put in Bell.

May laughed. 'You don't need to worry on that account. Anyone comes troubling us here, I'll put a barrel of buckshot into him!'

Matt saw from her expression that she meant it and could do it.

'We can look after the animals,'

Bethany said. She smiled shyly at the brothers.

Inkpen gave a quiet laugh. 'I got a right good family here,' he said to the brothers. 'Why don't we just go out there and pick up on the signs?'

Steve Inkpen and the brothers went out and looked for recent hoofprints and horse droppings. The old man knelt down close to the barn and examined boot marks.

'Could be nothing,' he speculated, 'but lookee here.' He pointed at bootprints close to the entrance of the barn. 'I guess this is where one of them stood when you came up on him. Would that be right?'

Matt knelt down beside him. 'Could be,' he said.

Steve Inkpen stood up and began to circle round. He had obviously been no mean tracker in his day. First he found the remains of the flaming torch that Joe had kicked away from the barn. Then he picked up more boot marks that seemed to match those at the entrance of the barn.

'Here we go,' he said. 'This is where they mounted up and rode away. Like you said, there must have some six of them. And lookee here, signs say they rode back in the direction of Dodge.' He stood up and grinned. 'That was a damned fool thing to do, wasn't it?'

'Must think we're too dumb to follow,' Joe said.

'Well, boys, if you want your horses back that's where we must go,' Steve Inkpen told them.

4

It was just before noon when they rode into Dodge City. Steve Inkpen was leading the way. Despite his advanced years he was still straight-backed in the saddle, and eagle-eyed, and he had the old fire in his belly. He had strapped on his gunbelt, had a Peacemaker in his holster and a Winchester carbine in its sheath close to his saddle.

'What do we aim to do?' Joe asked him.

The old man ran his hand through his walrus moustache and tweaked the end as though it helped him to think more clearly.

'Well, boys, the first thing we do is we go see Sheriff Potter. He might not be up to the standard of Bat Masterson and Wyatt Earp but he's a passable good man all the same and he has a string of deputies, most of them

86

ex-gunfighters who've come over to the law. He should be in his office or out there patrolling the boardwalk.'

They found the sheriff, a man called Luke Potter, ensconced in his office conferring with one of the deputies. Potter didn't look anything like the traditional lawman. In fact, he was more like a businessman or a city gent. He wore a bowler hat and a dark suit with a high-cut jacket with only the top button done up. In his vest he had a gold chain attached to an elegant gold watch. His legs were propped up on his desk. When Steve walked in the sheriff's eyes popped open.

'Why, good morning, my friend. What brings you here so early in the day?'

'Villainy!' Steve growled. 'Downright villainy. That's what brings me here.'

'That so?' Potter looked at him and grinned. 'Why, sure,' he said. 'What kind of villainy would that be?'

'The sort that comes to a man in the night and tries to burn his house down,'

Steve Inkpen complained.

'Why don't you tell me about it, Steve?' The sheriff took his legs off his desk and rearranged himself on his chair. 'Why don't you boys just take seats and tell me what happened?'

The deputy, a man called Christopher Chiplen, half-rose from his chair and then sat down again.

Steve sat opposite the sheriff and told his story. The two brothers sat a little to the right close to the deputy, who was dressed in a similar way to the sheriff.

Steve told the sheriff about the events of the night in some detail. Then he turned to the brothers and said, 'If it hadn't been for these two boys we might have been roasted alive in our beds.'

The sheriff raised his eyebrows a tad. 'You know who these *hombres* were?'

'We have a pretty good idea,' Matt said. Then he explained how Abe Benjamin and his sidekicks had robbed them at gunpoint by the riverside and stolen their horses.

'Yeah,' said the deputy, 'I saw you last evening riding into town on that old hoss of yours.'

'All we had,' Joe commented.

'You hear tell of Abe Benjamin?' Steve asked the sheriff.

Luke Potter grinned. 'Heard you tell of him — more than once, too,' he said. 'He was one of the scumbags you put inside the jailhouse some years back.'

Steve nodded grimly. 'Well, it seems he's risen from the dead and come back to haunt us. I just wanted to enquire: did he by any chance ride into town with his sidekicks early this morning?'

'With two extra horses,' Matt added.

The sheriff eyed them up and down. 'He might have done. This is a busy town and we can't check on everything. As long as people keep the peace we don't bother with them too much.'

'As long as they keep the peace,' the deputy added. 'And I see you boys are tooled up. I'm sure you know the rules in Dodge. We don't like men carrying firearms within the town limits.'

'Did you tell Abe Benjamin that?' Steve demanded.

Chris Chiplen grinned and looked at the sheriff.

Luke Potter looked at Steve Inkpen. 'Now Steve, I know how you must feel, specially after what happened last night, but it's my duty to add to what deputy Chiplen says: we have a peaceable town here and we aim to keep it that way.'

Steve Inkpen got up from his chair, looking somewhat aggrieved. 'I understand what you're saying, Sheriff, but I have my rights too.'

'You sure do,' Luke Potter said. 'And I'd be the first to support you in that.'

Steve Inkpen and the brothers stepped out of the sheriff's office. Matt looked at Inkpen and saw by his twitching moustaches and his blood suffused face that he was really riled up.

'Damned yellow belly!' Steve said. 'Just wanted to sit behind that desk and put his feet up. About as much use as a law enforcer as a pail of pig swill at a dinner table. And that deputy isn't much better either. Just as long as they got those bowler hats on straight they don't give a damn about anybody else!'

'What do we do now?' Joe asked him.

'What we do is we ride down to the Long Branch saloon and make a few enquiries.' The old man was so outraged he had difficulty in mounting his horse. So Matt got behind him and hefted him up.

They rode together down Main Street. The ex-marshal greeted friends on either side. He was obviously well-known and popular in town.

Between the sheriff's office and the saloon there was a large livery stable where they looked after horses and rented some out.

Steve Inkpen dismounted and tied his horse to the hitching-rail. The two brothers did likewise. Then they all went inside.

'Hi there, Tom!' Steve Inkpen called to a man giving the horses their feed.

'Why, Steve, what brings you in here?' came the reply. The man who emerged from the shadows was old but somewhat younger than Steve.

'Just making a few enquiries,' Steve said.

'Like in your old job, eh, Steve?' the man called Tom replied.

Steve Inkpen stroked his moustaches. 'Just wanted to know if you've seen a bunch of strangers, five or six, with two extra horses in tow?'

Tom scratched his bald pate. 'Now you come to mention it, Steve, I did see a bunch of men early this morning and they did have two extra horses. Nothing unusual about that.'

'Unless they happened to be stolen horses,' Matt said.

Tom gave him a sly look. 'Yes, well, I don't know about that.'

'What did the two trailing horses look like?' Joe asked him.

'Nothing special. Dun, I believe with blazes.' He paused. 'But I did notice one thing. They were both saddle horses. It did strike me as strange, those spare horses should have their own saddles just like the owners had fallen vanished.'

'Vanished, my arse!' Steve Inkpen exploded. 'Those two horses more than likely belonged to these young fellows.' He jerked his head towards the brothers.

'Yes, well,' Tom said. 'And now I do remember something else.'

'What's that?' Matt asked him.

Tom wrinkled his nose. 'One of those guys rode off shortly afterwards with those two horses in tow. It did seem kind of strange.'

'Thank you, Tom,' Inkpen said. 'I wonder just where those skookums went.'

'Did you happen to look into the Long Branch saloon, by any chance?' Tom asked.

'Oh, we'll be looking,' Steve said. 'That's my usual watering hole, as you probably know.'

They rode on down Main Street, none of them saying much. The two brothers were relying on the ex-marshal to guide them, and, though he had calmed down somewhat, he was still smouldering a little.

When they reached the Long Branch things were quiet, though the waiter who had served them the evening before was hovering about near the counter and a group of gamblers were playing poker. It looked as though they had been there all night trying to outbid each other.

Matt looked over at them and noted that none of the Abe Benjamin gang was present.

'What can I do for you, Mr Inkpen?' the waiter enquired, somewhat over-politely.

'You see six *hombres* in here earlier?' Steve asked him.

'A man called Abe and his sidekicks?' Joe added.

The waiter's eyes darted round nervously. 'No, sir, we haven't seen them in here. Why don't you try Bauder and Lauber's saloon, or the Crystal?'

Steve Inkpen nodded. 'Thank you, Warrender. That might be helpful.'

'It's a pleasure, Mr Inkpen, and I hope we have the honour of seeing you later.'

'You might just do that, Warrender, after we've concluded our business.' He turned to the brothers. 'I think we might investigate the Bauder and Lauber place. All fancy mirrors and polished bars. Too elaborate for me, but who knows?'

*   *   *

They went out to the horses, but before they could mount up they heard a shot.

'Hello!' Steve Inkpen said. 'There's some kind of ruckus going on down there. That should wake up Luke Potter and his deputy in a hurry!' He drew his Winchester from its sheath and started on down Main Street towards the Bauder and Lauber saloon.

Through the dust of the street Matt saw several hazy figures riding towards him, firing their guns as they came.

'Get under cover, boys!' Steve Inkpen shouted as he took shelter behind a barrel on the sidewalk. The brothers drew their Colt Frontiers and crouched down, ready for action. As the riders came on Joe popped his head up.

'Why, that's them!' he declared. 'I see Abe Benjamin, and he's shooting every which way.'

Steve Inkpen wasn't asking questions. He got up from behind his water barrel, levelled his Winchester, and fired. But it was a quick shot and he missed.

'Drat it!' he said as Abe Benjamin rode right past, firing a shot as he went. Then came the rest of the bunch, one, two, three, four. Steve Inkpen levelled his Winchester again and fired. The last of the bunch pitched back and fell.

A man came crawling towards them along the sidewalk. 'My God!' he was shouting. 'We've been robbed. They held up the bank.'

Then came Luke Potter in his black suit and bowler and he was now carrying a gun.

'Did you see them?' he shouted.

Then Chris Chiplen sprinted towards them and stopped, panting like a grampus.

Matt and Joe ran out on to Main

Street and looked down at the man Steve Inkpen had shot.

'That's the funny guy,' Joe said.

Matt looked down at the man's face. 'Well, he doesn't look too funny now.'

They would never know the humorist's name, nor hear any more of his jokes because he was well and truly dead. Yet, even in death he had a grin on his face; or was it a grimace of pain?

'You did a very fine job there,' Luke Potter admitted. 'Pity I had to shoot that *hombre*.'

The two brothers looked at one another in astonishment but said nothing. Steve Inkpen was in no mood to contradict anyone.

'Come into the Long Branch and have a whiskey on me,' Potter offered generously.

'No time for that,' Steve said. 'We got to get after those skookums, shoot the daylights out of them.'

Chris Chiplen had been into the bank and taken notes in his official notebook. Fortunately, nobody in the bank had been injured, though one of the tellers had fainted and had had to have cold water thrown over him to help him to revive.

'It all happened so quickly,' the manager said. 'One minute everything was going normally. The next minute those roughens were holding their guns on us and demanding the cash.'

'Did they get away with much?' Chiplen enquired.

'Several thousand dollars!' the manager said, aghast. 'We had to load up a bag with it. I thought this was a peaceable town.'

'Don't you worry, sir,' Chiplen said. 'Those men will be brought to justice. I can promise you that.'

Outside the Long Branch saloon everything was in disarray. Even the over-polite waiter had his mouth open in dismay.

Now Steve Inkpen's old instincts as a marshal kicked in. 'Get on your horses, boys. We're going after those skookums before they get clean away.'

Matt pushed him up into the saddle and mounted the horse he had borrowed from the ex-marshal back at the ranch; Joe quickly followed suit.

'Wait on me,' Luke Potter shouted as they pulled out on to Main Street.

Inkpen turned in the saddle. 'No time for that!' he shouted. 'You follow on as fast as you can!' Then he urged his mount forward in a gallop.

The two horses the brothers were riding were good stock and seemed to enjoy a gallop.

We're gonna catch up with those sons of bitches, Matt thought as his horse leaped over the ground. The Abe Benjamin bunch couldn't be far ahead. He could smell the sweat of the horses and see the occasional horsedung. Following their trail was a cinch.

But there would be complications. These began when the country started to break up and they were riding between a series of low buttes.

Steve Inkpen held up his hand and they drew to a halt. The ex-marshal looked down at the trail and read the signs. Then he pointed up at a butte.

'They're up here somewhere, boys,' he said. 'I think they aim to make a stand. Ride carefully. These hombres are as tricky as rattlesnakes and three times as deadly. So tread carefully. We don't want to lose anybody, do we?'

Before he could move on up among the rocks Luke Potter and Chris Chiplen caught up with them. They looked somewhat incongruous, just like city gents in their dark suits and their bowler hats, but they did have their gunbelts strapped on.

'What's happening, Marshal?' Luke Potter asked. 'Have you lost them already?'

Steve Inkpen squinted up at the butte. 'They're up there somewhere, Mr Potter, and, like cornered rats, they're ready to kill. So you'd better keep your heads down if you don't want them blown off your necks.'

'Me and Chris will circle round and cut off their retreat,' Potter said.

'Good idea,' the ex-marshal agreed, 'just as long as you don't mistake us for the villains.'

Luke Potter and Chris Chiplen rode away towards the other side of the butte.

'And a damn good riddance to them,' Steve muttered. He turned to the brothers. 'Can you two boys shoot with those popguns of yours?'

'I think we're good enough,' Matt assured him.

'Pity you haven't got Winchesters or Springfields,' Inkpen said. 'Longer range and more accurate.'

'Well, we must do our best then,' Matt said.

They dismounted and tethered their horses to some low scrub growing among the rocks.

'Can't be far ahead,' Steve Inkpen said. 'It's awful rough on horses up there. They'll be cut to pieces. So spread out, boys, and advance with caution. My guess is that they're up there, ahead of us.' He pointed at the high crest of the butte. 'That would be the best shooting point — something like a fort up there.'

'You think we can take it?' Joe asked him.

'Sure we can take it,' the ex-marshal said. 'You want your horses back, don't you?'

Before the brothers could reply a shot was fired from above. The bullet ricocheted off a rock close to Steve Inkpen's head, sending up a shower of splintered rock.

The three of them ducked down quickly.

'That was a close call,' Joe said.

The ex-marshal raised his head a little and peered up towards the crest of the butte, not too far away. 'I think that was probably a Springfield,' he said. 'Unless I'm mistaken they're up there, where I said. Pity I haven't got my spyglass with me. The guy with that gun certainly knows his business.'

'What do you suggest, Marshal?' Matt asked. Steve Inkpen studied the lie of the land.

'They went up this way,' he said. 'Easier on the horses. What we do is split up and advance cautiously. Joe, why don't you go off to the right there? You see that rock up there, shaped like an ass's head?'

'I see it.'

'Then why don't you make your way up there, good and quiet. Try not to displace too many rocks. We don't want to start an avalanche here, do we?'

He turned to Matt. 'And why don't you go left and make your way up there? I'm going up by the centre route if my old bones can make it. If you boys can keep me in sight. I'll make hand signals so you know what I'm going to do.' He made simple suggestions about the hand signals he would make but Matt noticed that he was out of breath and puffing; his face had an unhealthy tinge to it.

'You all right, Marshal?' he asked.

'Shall be when I catch my breath,' Steve Inkpen gasped. But he was far from all right. In fact, at that moment, he was all wrong. He clung to the rock, slid down it and rolled over on to his back.

Matt reached out and caught him before he could hit the rocky ground too hard.

'You OK, sir?' he said quietly.

'I guess I got too excited,' the old man declared. 'I don't think I can go on, dammit. You boys'll just have to go on without me. Take the Winchester and do what you can to stop those villains from getting away with it.' Now his breath became more laboured and he pressed his hand to his side. 'Damn pain in my side,' he groaned.

Matt and Joe exchanged looks of concern.

'What do we do?' Joe asked.

'We stay and take care of him,' Matt replied.

Steven Inkpen waved his hand feebly. 'Leave me, leave me,' he said. 'Get after those skunks and bring them to justice like I said.' He grimaced with pain, then closed his eyes and lost consciousness.

'My God! I think he's going,' Joe said. 'What can we do?'

Matt didn't reply. He had straddled the old man and was pumping down on Steve's ribs as he had seen his pa demonstrate years before.

Joe stood up and looked around as though he expected someone to be close enough to offer help. But there was nobody within sight or sound. The sheriff and his deputy had disappeared.

'Listen, Joe, go down and get your horse and ride back to town. Get a buckboard or something and bring it back so that we can get the old man to town so the doctor can work on him.'

'Sure, sure,' Joe said in something of a panic. 'Is he gonna be OK?'

'He's still breathing,' Matt said, none too hopefully.

Joe nodded and broke away. As he was scrambling down towards the horses someone fired a shot from above, but fortunately it missed by a yard.

'You bastards will have to wait,' Matt muttered between clenched teeth.

* * *

Joe untethered his horse, mounted up and rode like hell back into town. It seemed much closer than he had expected. As he drew near to the town a dozen riders came riding towards him. When he came up to them one of them drew rein.

'What happened?' the man asked. 'Did you catch up on them?'

'No!' Joe shouted. 'We need help. The old man had a heart attack or something. He's lying there and Matt's trying to keep him alive.'

'You mean they got away?' another man shouted.

'Did Steve get shot?' a third man asked.

'No,' Joe shouted again. 'He had some kind of attack. I've got to get back to town and find help.'

'OK, boys,' the leader said. 'Chester, you ride back with the man and get help. The rest of us will ride on and try to catch those bank robbers.'

The riders pulled away in a cloud of dust, leaving Joe with the man called Chester.

'OK,' Chester said. 'I'll take you to Doc Mason. We'll get a wagon and bring it out. 'You think the old man's gonna survive?'

'Well, he doesn't look too healthy at the moment,' Joe said with concern.

They rode back into town. Chester led Joe to Doc Mason's place and left him there while he went to fetch a buckboard. Joe burst in on the doc's place, just as the doc was drinking a morning coffee with his wife. Doc Mason looked up in astonishment and was about to complain, but Joe cut him off without apology and told him what had happened.

'You mean Steve's been taken sick?' Mason said. 'I'd better come right away.' He was thrusting things into his bag as he spoke.

In less than a minute they were mounted and galloping in the direction of the incident. As they rode they passed Chester and another man who was driving the buckboard.

When Joe and Doc Mason got close to Matt they saw that he was down on one knee looking at Steve Inkpen. Inkpen actually had his eyes open. The doc dismounted, ran to the patient and bent down to examine the ex-marshal.

Steve Inkpen turned his head slightly to look at the doc.

'So, you're here, Doc,' he croaked. 'I think I strained myself deep inside. Can't seem to move and everything's gone dim.'

Doc Mason frowned. 'Get something under his head,' he said. 'Make him as comfortable as possible.'

'I'd like to get up on my horse,' Steve muttered weakly, 'but I don't think I can make it.'

'You just lie still,' the doc told him. He turned to Matt. 'Get something to cover him with. But don't try to move him.'

Chester was now just below them with the buckboard, but he hadn't thought to bring a blanket. So Doc Mason stripped off his coat and laid it on the sick man.

Steve Inkpen tried to smile. 'Thanks,' he said.

It was the last thing he said. The next moment he shuddered and gasped, stretched out and died.

They carried the dead man to the buckboard and laid him down, taking care to treat him respectfully. It would be a bumpy ride back to Dodge City but Steve Inkpen wasn't about to complain. He was past all complaining now.

'What will you do?' Doc Mason asked the brothers. Matt and Joe looked at one another.

'I guess we'll ride back to town,' Matt said.

'I think so,' Joe agreed.

Neither of them had the heart to ride on after the bank robbers. *Funny how things fall into perspective when someone dies*, Matt thought. *The whole world seems nothing but an empty farce.*

'Anyway,' Joe said, 'we met a posse as we rode into town. They will pick up the trail and should catch up on the sheriff fast enough.'

So they escorted the body on the buckboard like an armed escort. When they reached the outskirts of town people came out to gape at the ex-marshal's body. The doctor had closed Steve's eyes and he looked strangely at peace, considering the circumstances.

5

Jake's funeral parlour was quite a thriving business in Dodge at that time. The owner, a man called Jake Lorimer, had set up shop with his wife shortly after arriving in Dodge City twenty years before and they had soon become surprisingly prosperous. Quite apart from all the villains on both sides of the law who had been laid to rest in the town graveyard, they had an excellent clientele. Now they could afford a black hearse with fancy gold curlicues engraved on the doors. This chariot of death was drawn by two black horses with dark cockades to convey their most well-to-do customers to the grave.

But Jake and his wife were democrats, who claimed to respect the dead of every class, even the bad men and women who had been shot down on the street in gunfights. One such man, the humorist member of Abe Benjamin's gang that had robbed the bank was lying in a coffin in the back room with his arms crossed piously across his chest, waiting to be transported to the common burial ground which some people had dubbed Boot Hill.

But ex-marshal Steve Inkpen was a well-respected gent. So he was worthy of special treatment — the best the establishment could offer. Matt and Joe knew that the old man was popular but they had no idea just how popular he had been. And nobody knew for certain how old he was, either. Some even claimed he was eighty years old, but that was an exaggeration since his daughters were just eighteen and twenty, so it seemed problematical, though most agreed that he must be close to seventy. And his wife was some fifteen years his junior.

When they brought his body back to the city, Doc Mason looked at Matt and said:

'What are we going to do about May, the widow? Maybe I should ride out and give her the sad news.'

Matt shook his head. 'I think we could do that, Doc. We haven't been here long but we feel we know them pretty well already.'

The doc looked relieved. 'Well, I'm grateful for that but Marshal Inkpen had a lot of friends here in Dodge, and he was a good man. So maybe I should ride out with you.'

Everyone agreed to that. If a whole bunch of people arrived at the Inkpen spread the womenfolk would think the world had come to an end, which in a way it had: at least for them.

But before they could set out, something else occurred. Sheriff Luke Potter and his deputy Christopher Chiplen limped back into town. Chiplen's head was leaning forward over his saddle and he was bleeding profusely. They helped him down from his horse and carried him into what served as Doc Mason's surgery. The other men in the posse looked somewhat defeated.

'Had to let those varmints go,' the

leader of the posse reported. 'They gunned down on us and Chiplen caught one in the shoulder. So we thought we must get back to save his life.'

When Joe told them about the ex-marshal's death from a probable heart attack, they were dumbfounded.

'Who'd have thought it?' a member of the posse said. 'A man like that!'

'Maybe we should ride out and let the widow know,' the leader of the posse remarked.

'That's all in hand,' Doc Mason informed him.

Sheriff Luke Potter looked strangely forlorn and subdued in his battered black bowler hat.

* * *

Matt and Joe rode back to the Inkpen spread alone, the doc being too busy treating Christopher Chiplen's wound. The bullet from the Sharps had caught him high in the shoulder and splintered the bone. Chiplen was lucky to be alive, but he would be out of action for a good long time.

'What are we gonna say to them?' Joe asked as they rode back to the spread.

'We tell them the truth,' Matt replied.

'What, everything?'

'Not everything,' Matt said. 'Just enough to tell them the old man died bravely. They'll want to know the details later. When they see us riding in on our own they'll probably draw their own conclusions.'

When they drew near to the spread they saw the two young women working on the lot close to the ranch house. Annabelle was tilling between the vegetables, Bethany was feeding the hens; and the hens were squabbling and fussing all round her like old maids at a party.

As the brothers approached the two girls straightened up and looked towards them expectantly. Their mother appeared at the door with her shotgun. She gave the brothers a hard stare with her searching grey eyes.

'She knows,' Joe said quietly.

The younger daughter, Bethany, looked at the brothers anxiously.

'Where's pa?' she called out.

'You'd better do the talking,' Joe said to Matt.

Matt dismounted. 'Mrs Inkpen,' he said, 'I'm afraid we bring bad news.'

May Inkpen shook her head. 'What happened?'

'We're sorry to tell you the marshal passed away,' Matt said.

'Was he shot?' she asked abruptly.

'No, ma'am. He overstrained himself. We did our best for him but we couldn't save him. Right now, his body's lying in Jake's funeral parlour.'

May Inkpen shook her head again, but there was no sign of a tear. Annabelle stood aghast and Bethany covered her face with her shawl.

These are brave frontier women, Matt thought.

★   ★   ★

They gave Steve Inkpen a grand funeral. Not quite fit for a king, perhaps, but good enough for a man highly respected in the community. Someone had actually rustled up the town band, which consisted of a trumpet player, a trombonist, a fiddle player, and a guy in a bobble hat who did his best with a squeezebox. The outfit was almost in tune but for the fact that the trumpeter played one or two flat notes and the fiddler seemed somewhat unsure of his instrument. Several voices in the crowd who wailed like banshees added to the tone of pathos. The whole community seemed to have turned out, including the staff from the saloon. Which made it quite an event!

Matt and Joe had been given the privilege of residence in the Long Branch for the few days before the funeral and a local tailor had rigged them out in dark suits, so that they were able to act as pall-bearers, together with two other young notables.

Indeed, Annabelle and Bethany had wanted to be involved as pall-bearers, but May deemed that to be somewhat undignified for ladies. So they just watched the coffin being carried into the cramped interior of the building that served as a church. The minister delivered a wearisome eulogy on the dead man, describing him as one of the greatest lawmen in Kansas and maybe the whole of the American western states. When he started using phrases like 'this great country of ours' and 'we must walk together in dignity' the brothers exchanged glances and raised their eyebrows.

After the funeral everyone seemed to have worked up a raging appetite. The owners of the Long Branch saloon, of which Steve Inkpen had been a regular customer, laid on quite a feast, and the food was somewhat better than the crappy stuff that Steve Inkpen had condemned.

Everyone had behaved with appropriate decorum in the little church, but when they piled into the Long Branch saloon, their mood changed abruptly and people started chattering away like monkeys in a zoo.

Sheriff Luke Potter sidled up to Matt and Joe and placed a hand on Joe's shoulder.

'I want to thank you two boys for keeping your heads and taking such good care of our friend in his last moments.'

Joe smiled. 'We did what anyone would have done,' he said. Matt nodded as the sheriff turned towards him.

'You boys have plans for the future?' Potter asked.

'Nothing special,' Matt said.

'Well, I could do with a couple of deputies like you and I'm sure the town council will support me on that. It seems that my deputy Chris might be out of service for quite some time.' He gave the two brothers a look of enquiry.

Matt said, 'Thank you, Mr Potter. We'll think on the matter.'

'Do that, my boy, do that.' Potter

gave Matt a patronizing pat on the shoulder and turned away to offer condolences to the widow.

There had been so many people in the little church, and it had been so gloomy, that Matt hadn't had time to pick out anyone in particular. Now he was surprised to see his old boss Ken Calloway threading his way towards them. Calloway had a gleam of humour in his eye.

'Why, howdy, Mr Calloway,' Joe said.

Calloway was looking at Matt, and Matt noted that he had a dark suit on and a gold chain across his vest, but he wasn't smoking his usual cigar.

'It seems you haven't travelled far since we last met,' the rancher said, with a more than a hint of irony.

'That's because things happened on the way,' Matt replied.

Calloway raised a shaggy grey eyebrow. 'What sort of things?'

Matt told him about Shamanzo and their encounter with Abe Benjamin and his gang. Calloway looked more than a little impressed.

'You mean you killed Shamanzo?'

'Had to,' Joe interjected. 'He was trying to kill us.'

Calloway nodded his head grimly. 'Shamanzo was a bully. I wondered where he'd gone when he quit the ranch. And you say the Benjamin gang stole your money and your horses?'

'We were bathing in the creek,' Joe explained. 'It could have happened to anyone.'

Calloway raised his head sceptically. 'And then you came to town and met my friend Steve Inkpen, who turned out to be something of a good fairy. Is that the story?'

'That's the truth,' Matt said.

'After which the Benjamin bunch shot up the Inkpen spread and then robbed the bank. Is that the way it goes?'

'That's what happened,' Joe said.

Calloway had retained his sceptical grin. 'It seems you boys have something of a jinx on you. Misfortune follows you like a shadow wherever you go. Would you say that'd be correct, gentlemen?'

'Well, I don't know about that, Mr Calloway,' Joe said defensively. 'You gave us dollars to help us along and we were robbed. That's what it amounts to.'

Calloway eyed him suspiciously. 'What do you aim to do now?' he asked. The brothers were silent for a moment.

'What we aim to do,' Matt said, 'is we meet our obligations.'

'How would that be?' the rancher asked.

'That would be that we still aim to track that rustler Ned Shanklin and his gang. You want his head on a plate and we'll give it to you as best we can.'

For the first time Calloway gave a genuine smile.

'I believe you will,' he said, stretching out his hand. 'I do believe you will.'

'That's a big promise,' Joe said to Matt as the rancher walked away.

'Obligation,' Matt replied, tight-lipped.

* * *

It's surprising how the guests melt away after a funeral and the refreshments. Nobody likes to hang about too long in case he feels the horny hand of the Angel of Death on his shoulder, or someone might even ask for a contribution towards the funeral costs! Soon the Long Branch saloon was almost empty, except for the poker players who were drifting towards their usual tables. Matt concluded that they might even continue their incessant poker game in hell and never notice the difference.

'Has it occurred to you, brother,' Joe said, 'that we have no more than a cent between us and nowhere to rest our heads?'

' "Even the foxes have holes",' Matt quoted.

'And that makes things difficult,' Joe added with a grin. 'What d'you think we should do?'

But Matt had no time to reply because he looked up and saw Annabelle approaching them. For a moment she said nothing and Matt saw she had a look of caution in her eye.

'Mother wanted me to say thank you,' she said after a moment.

'We don't need thank yous,' he said. 'It was a pleasure to meet your pa and be of some service to your family.'

Annabelle gave a slight bob. 'Mother has asked me to give you an invitation.'

Matt and Joe waited. 'That's very kind,' Joe said.

Annabelle blushed slightly. 'You're to come back to the ranch and stay until you've decided about your future.'

There was another silence. Matt looked directly at Annabelle and she gave an almost imperceptible nod.

'Well, thank you, ma'am,' he said. 'Tell your mother we'll be more than glad to accept her kind invitation.'

The brothers followed the buggy, driven by May Inkpen, back to the Inkpen ranch.

'So the foxes found holes after all,' Joe said to Matt.

Matt made no reply. He was deep in thought. It was as though the ground beneath him was shifting slightly and he couldn't understand which way it would settle.

When the buggy pulled up outside the ranch May turned towards them and said:

'Come right inside, boys. After today you'll always be welcome in this home.'

The two brothers walked into the spick and span room, which smelled of polish and other strange, indefinable scents. They stood with their hats in their hands, not knowing quite what to say.

'Girls, take the gentlemen's hats,' May said. 'Show them we care for good manners here.' Though she spoke with a kind of roughness, her eyes shone with gratitude.

The daughters came forward, bobbed and took the brothers' Stetsons.

'Now, gentlemen,' May said, 'I want you to make yourselves at home here. Please sit down at the table and we'll talk about the future.'

What future? Matt wondered. The brothers sat down in the places they had occupied on the night before Steve Inkpen died. The girls sat opposite them. May took up position on the left of the table. The other end, where Steve Inkpen usually sat, was left empty.

Matt heard the slow, solemn tick of the great clock and thought that the ghost of Steve Inkpen might be sitting there, smiling to himself and wondering what might be said next.

May Inkpen fidgeted with her hands and looked strangely nervous for a moment, then she gathered her strength. She looked up quickly and said:

'The fact is, we need your help.'

Matt and Joe glanced at one another briefly.

'How come?' Joe said.

Both girls were staring down at their hands on the table, looking more than a little embarrassed.

Matt nodded. 'Well, we're listening, Mrs Inkpen, and we're always glad to be of help. So why don't you tell us what we can do?'

May Inkpen had a sad smile on her face. 'I have to tell you something you might already have suspected.'

The brothers said nothing. Matt was looking at Annabelle and he saw that her lips trembled slightly, and that made the ground under him shift a little more.

'The fact is,' May said after a pause, 'my husband wasn't all he seemed to be.'

Matt looked down the table towards her; their eyes met and something like understanding seemed to come between them.

'You met him in the Long Branch saloon,' she said. 'And that's where he was most days. He drank a lot and treated other people to drinks. You could say he was an over-generous man.'

'He sure was generous to us, ma'am,' Joe put in.

'The trouble is, he was far too generous,' May said. 'He spent more money than he had. That's why . . . ' She almost choked on the last words and Bethany got up from the table to comfort her.

Now Annabelle spoke out loud and clear. 'The fact is, we're on the verge of bankruptcy,' she said bravely. 'We can work hard but we haven't the time to clear Father's debts.' Before she could go on, May spoke up again.

'Don't misunderstand us, gentlemen. He was a good man but he couldn't deal with money. So he got depressed and the more depressed he got the more he drank and the more he drank the deeper he got into depression.'

'But he was so bright and cheerful,' Joe said.

'Yes,' May agreed. 'Even depressed folk can be bright and cheerful on the outside.'

'OK,' Matt said. 'You want us to help you build up the spread. Is that what you would like, Mrs Inkpen?'

May smiled and nodded. 'I know Steve trusted you two young men. He spoke very highly of you. I won't tell you what he said but I know he thought very highly of you. And another thing you should know, I have no money to pay you and you'll have to go on sleeping in the barn if you choose to stay on. I know it will be awful cold out there come winter but we'll cross that bridge when we come to it.' Matt and Joe glanced at one another.

Joe said, 'We're nothing but two cow-punchers, ma'am. I hope you understand that.'

Matt stirred himself and thought he felt the ground under him beginning to settle a little.

'Well, Mrs Inkpen, your husband was generous to us. So I think we'll stay.'

The girls looked up and May Inkpen began to smile through her tears.

* * *

'What in hell's name did you say that for?' Joe said when they were alone in the barn.

'What would you have said?' Matt retorted.

Joe fell silent. He had considered the

options and they didn't look too rosy. They hadn't two bits to rub together between them. They could have gone back to the home farm and worked their bones off for their father. They could go back to Calloway and ask him to take them on again, mending fences and riding nighthawk on the herds. They might even take to robbing banks. That was what a lot of impoverished cowpokes took to when they were laid off. Joe might have considered it himself if he hadn't had his brother Matt to contend with; and sometimes Matt was like an old-time Puritan.

Then he thought about those two girls, especially the apple-cheeked Bethany.

He looked at his brother and said: 'I think you said right, Matt. It was the best of a bum deal, specially since we haven't a hope in hell of finding out where Ned Shanklin keeps his rustled cattle.'

Matt smiled. 'I don't know about that,' he said. He looked up as though waiting for the gods to speak.

All through to late summer the brothers worked their socks off on the farm. Though they had never thought of themselves as sodbusters they even began to enjoy the work. Joe mainly helped with the livestock and Matt assisted Annabelle in tilling the soil. The Inkpen women had a small patch of wheat from which they hoped to produce their own bread. But the soil was poor and, despite their hard work, the harvest was likely to be meagre.

One bright morning Matt and Annabelle paused to refresh themselves with a swig of cheesy-tasting beer from a large jug that May brought out to them. Matt looked round at the spread and felt something like one of those Old Testament prophets he had read about.

Annabelle, or Bell as she preferred to be called, stood beside him and passed the stone jar over to him. He accepted the jug and took a long swig from the lip where hers had touched it. Bell watched him and smiled: she had a smile just like her father's, bright and cheerful like the sun coming out of a cloud.

'I don't know what we're going to do, but we're not going to win,' she said.

Matt looked at her and nodded. 'I think you're right, Miss Bell.'

She pursed her lips. 'That's one thing I like about you, Matt,' she said. 'You don't care for lies and you tell the truth.'

He looked at her steadily for a moment and felt the ground sway slightly under his feet.

'The truth is all we've got, Miss Bell.' He straightened his back. 'And you're right, we can't win here. The soil is too poor. We might spread a few of cowpats and horse apples on it, but we can't win. You know that and I know that.'

She looked at him and frowned. 'I have another thought, Mr Stowe.'

'And what is that, Miss Bell?'

She regarded him gravely for a moment. 'I don't put you down as a settling man, Mr Stowe. I put you down as a restless spirit. Sooner or later you'll feel the call to move on and make your fortune in some other way.'

Matt raised his eyebrows and looked up at the clouds.

'You could be right, Miss Bell. I am restless and I guess it's the way I'm made. But right now I'm content to stay.'

'What about winter?' she asked. 'It can be bitter here in winter.'

'Winter's a couple of months away,' he said. He was leaning on his spade. When the sun was shining it was still quite warm, but when the wind swept across the plains they felt the breath of bitter cold shivering on their cheeks. 'Sure, we have to think about the future but right now we're in the present and we've got to get the harvest in.'

Yet, as he spoke, the words sounded hollow in his ears. What do you do for a lost cause? he wondered. Do you stick around and go down with the sinking ship, hoping someone will throw you a lifebelt, or dive overboard and swim for the shore? Which sounded like a good metaphor but didn't make a lot of sense if you didn't know where the dry land lay.

★ ★ ★

Joe was cleaving logs when two men came riding in on a buggy. Bethany looked up quickly and saw them.

'My God, it's them!' she gasped.

'Who's them?' Joe said.

'That's the man from the bank, Mr Brewer, and the other one is Chepland, the surveyor.'

The buggy drew up in front of the ranch house. The two men raised their tall hats and clambered down.

'Well, now, Miss Bethany, or is it Miss Annabelle?' The man from the bank gave a deep rumbling chuckle. You can often read a man's nature by the way he laughs, and though Joe wasn't particularly proficient in psychology he knew there was something he didn't like about that laugh.

Now May appeared from behind the house where she had been chasing a hen to cook for dinner. She was wiping her hands on her apron, which somehow she contrived to keep clean.

'Good afternoon, Mr Brewer,' she said with a kind of wary courtesy.

'Afternoon,' the banker said, sweeping off his tall hat. 'Thought we'd just drop by and see how you are, Mrs Inkpen.'

'Terrible thing that happened to your husband,' the surveyor said, looking round at the property. 'See you've got hired up now.' His eyes rested on Joe.

'We're just helping out of friendship,' Joe said. May looked at the two men, then at Joe.

'Why don't you come inside and have yourselves a glass?' she invited.

'Well, thank you, ma'am. I believe we will.'

The banker and the surveyor followed May into the cabin.

'Vipers!' Beth said to Joe.

Joe looked at her enquiringly. She

lowered her voice.

'They drink Mother's beer but they've come to suck her blood.'

'How come?' Joe asked.

'The mortgage money is due and we haven't got the dollars. That man Brewer wants to foreclose on the property and drive us out.' She spoke with surprising bitterness for a such a sweet-natured young woman. Joe thought of the chill of the winter that was to come and almost shivered.

'He can't do that, can he?'

'I'm afraid he can,' Beth said. 'Like Mother said, Pa was foolish with money, so he mortgaged the farm for money to spend on the easy life. That's what Pa was like.'

* * *

Matt and Bell had seen the buggy arrive and they started for the cabin. Bell also revealed the fact of her father's mortgage to Matt.

'You mean they can take the place off

you?' Matt said.

Bell nodded. 'That's how foolish Pa was,' she said. 'The fact is, we're mortgaged to the hilt.'

They walked back to the cabin but there was no room at the table. The banker and the surveyor were sitting there drinking May's cheesy beer out of huge tankards. Brewer raised his glass like a toast to Matt and Bell as they arrived.

'Why, greetings!' he said in his deep tone.

Matt nodded. Like Joe, he didn't take to the banker. Indeed, he remembered Brewer standing hat in hand at Steve Inkpen's graveside. It wasn't so much the laugh but the way Brewer had glanced round at the other mourners, almost like a ferret looking for a tame rabbit.

'So you boys are here to help the good ladies?' the banker said.

'Anyway we can, sir,' Matt replied.

'Well, that's good,' Brewer said. 'And we'd like to thank you both for looking after the marshal in his hour of need and also for trying to gun down on that Benjamin bunch after they robbed the bank.'

'We did our best,' Joe said.

Brewer was chuckling again. 'Just like the Good Samaritan, eh?' he speculated.

'We're not saints,' Matt replied. 'We're just men who work as hard as we can to earn our keep.'

'Well, that's mighty honest of you.' The banker rose from the table and tilted his tankard. 'And may you be rewarded for that.' He took a long slurp of his beer and sat down again. 'Real good beer this, Mrs Inkpen.'

He turned to Matt again. 'By the way, did you boys hear? We are offering a substantial reward for the apprehension of those robbers, dead or alive.'

Matt and Joe glanced at one another briefly.

'Dead or alive?' Joe queried.

'Why, yes indeed,' the banker said. 'Figure of speech. Naturally, we'd sooner see them behind bars than stretched out dead. But, of course, if they were dead they wouldn't be inclined to rob any more banks, would they?' After delivering what he considered to be a very witty joke, he threw back his head and gave a great bellowing laugh.

'Tell you what,' Brewer said to May. 'I want to be generous to you, Mrs Inkpen, especially after all you've been through lately.' He paused dramatically and looked round with his ferrety eyes. 'So I'll tell you what we'll do. I'm going to postpone your payment on the mortgage for this quarter. Who knows what might happen in the next month or two?'

Matt thought: *What will happen in the next month or two will be you'll double the interest and turn the screw on these womenfolk who won't know which way to turn.*

* * *

In the barn that night the brothers discussed the matter.

'We have to do something to help these women,' Joe said.

'What do you suggest?' Matt asked him.

Joe wrinkled his nose. 'We could rob a bank,' he said.

Matt laughed. 'You really think that would help?'

'It might if we got away with it.'

'Don't be a damned fool, Joe.'

Joe shook his head. 'There could be another way.'

'What would that be?'

'We could marry those two girls.'

Matt stared at him in surprise. 'Is that a serious suggestion?'

Joe grinned back. 'I kinda like Bethany and I do believe she likes me.'

Matt shook his head slowly. 'Liking isn't good enough,' he said. 'There has to be a lot more.'

'You really think so?' Joe was still grinning. 'I've seen the way Bell looks at you too and I know she's keen.'

Matt looked away and then came back. 'How would that help?'

'Help what?'

'Help keep the wolf from the farm?' Matt said.

Joe shrugged. 'It would show commitment, wouldn't it?' he said. 'Isn't that important?'

6

A week or so later Matt and Bell took the buggy into Dodge City to purchase supplies: flour, sugar, beans, and so on: the things they couldn't produce on the farm. May had written a list and given it to Bell, who she knew would be as frugal as she was. Out of courtesy Bell let Matt take the reins, and they sat side by side, almost shoulder to shoulder. Matt had a strange feeling of closeness he had never experienced before.

'Why do you carry that weapon?' Bell asked, looking down at the Colt Frontier strapped to Matt's side.

'That's because I'm learning, Miss Bell,' he said.

'But you're not a gunman,' she argued. 'You're a farmer.'

Matt smiled to himself. 'Well, I was a cowpuncher till recently and this gun has saved my life more than once. So I figure it's a good idea to have it by me . . . just in case. Your pa used a shooter for a living, I believe. In fact he was famous for it.'

He turned to her and thought he saw a tear trembling on her lashes. 'Sorry I mentioned that,' he said. 'It was downright insensitive.'

Now she was smiling again. 'You're not insensitive, Matt. In fact you might be a little too sensitive for your own good.'

He was still looking at her and thinking what a damned fine profile she had, almost willing her to turn her face towards him, but she looked away.

It was a short ride to Dodge and now they were on the outskirts. The store they wanted was some way along Main Street, next to the Long Branch saloon, but before they reached it they had to pass the sheriff's office. Sheriff Luke Potter was sitting on a rocking-chair on the edge of the sidewalk, catching the sun and surveying what he thought of as his kingdom. He looked up as the buggy approached and pushed his bowler hat back on his head.

'Why, Miss Annabelle!' he said. 'How nice to see you.' His eyes switched to Matt. 'You too, Mr Stowe. What brings you to town?' He was grinning suggestively at the pair sitting side by side like two birds on a fence.

'Just come in for supplies,' Bell said.

Potter made a sideways gesture with his head. 'Did you see the notice, Mr Stowe?'

'What notice would that be?'

'Notice for the Abe Benjamin's gang, dead or alive,' the sheriff said. 'They're offering quite a substantial reward. I've pinned it up there. You see it?'

Matt and Bell clambered down from the buggy and took a look at the poster the newspaper printers had printed. It said the local bankers were offering a $2,000 reward for the bank robbers. Underneath, there were artist's impressions of the four bandits. Matt peered closely at the faces depicted and chuckled.

'Well, I can tell you one thing, Mr

Potter: you're never going to run those skookums to ground if you look at those fancy pictures, because none of them look anything like that.'

'Artist's licence.' Potter laughed. He turned his head and peered at Matt. 'Have you thought about my offer, Mr Stowe?'

'What offer was that, Mr Potter?'

Potter held his head on one side. 'Don't play dumb, Mr Stowe. You remember damned well I offered to deputize you. Or have you got other things on your mind?' His lip curled suggestively as he looked at Bell. 'Begging your pardon, ma'am.'

Matt was thinking about the reward and the prospects of becoming a deputy sheriff. The pay wouldn't be much but he could at least use it to help to keep the Inkpen farm away from the jaws of the wolves.

'I'm still thinking about it,' he said. 'By the way, that reward, would it be for the whole bunch, or is it two thousand dollars a head?'

Potter laughed again. 'You should be so lucky,' he said.

Matt and Bell mounted the buggy again and rode on down to the store.

Bell was sucking her lower lip which might have been considered somewhat unlady-like, but Matt thought it was disturbingly attractive.

'Are you really thinking about that job?' she asked him.

He smiled. 'You have to think about everything, Miss Bell,' he replied enigmatically.

They were approaching the general store right next to the Long Branch saloon.

'Just a minute,' he said. He pulled the buggy to a halt outside the store. 'You see that saddle horse tethered to the rail outside the Long Branch?'

She drew in a breath. 'I see it.'

'Well, I'll be damned,' he said. 'That's my horse, the one Abe Benjamin's gang stole from me, unless I'm a Dutchman.'

They walked on down to the hitching

rail. The horse turned its head and snickered. Matt put out his hand and ran it through the horse's mane.

'Poor Sullivan,' he murmured. 'He looks kind of neglected. And look here . . . ' He now had his hand on the saddle. 'This is my saddle too. Look. it's got my initials MS engraved on it.' Bell looked close and saw that he was right.

'What are you going to do?'

'Well, first I'm going to take poor Sullivan to the livery stable and give him a feed and a drink. The poor beast looks half starved. Why don't you go into the store and make your purchases?'

'Well now,' Bell said, 'don't go getting yourself into trouble while I'm gone, will you?'

'Not if I can help it,' he promised.

He took the halter and led Sullivan down to the livery stable. The man in the livery stable greeted him warmly.

'Why, you're the young man who brought that poor dying man Marshal Inkpen into town right after those Abe

Benjamin boys had robbed the bank.'

'That is so,' Matt agreed, 'and this is the horse they stole from me.'

'Well, I'll be damned!' the man said.

'Did you happen to see who was riding Sullivan and where the *hombre* is now?'

'Oh, I saw right enough,' the man said. 'He fell right off this poor horse, pissed as a newt, out of his mind. Then he staggered into the saloon and collapsed, so I heard. I don't know where he is now.'

Matt walked down to the Long Branch saloon, where he was greeted immediately by the waiter who had served him that crap meal when he first rode into the city. The waiter looked pleased, even excited to welcome him.

'Ah, Mr Stowe, how good to see you. Can I get you a drink, sir, or maybe a snack of some sort?'

'Not at the moment,' Matt said. 'I'm looking for information.'

'Ah, yes, sir. What kind if information, sir?' The waiter was holding his hands together like a tame squirrel begging for nuts.

'A man rode in earlier this morning and he was so paralysed by drink that he fell off his horse. I believe they carried him in here so he could sober up.'

The waiter nodded eagerly. 'Yes, sir. I saw him myself. Very bad case of drunkenness. Very bad indeed.'

'So what happened to him?'

'Well, sir, he lay out there on the sidewalk for quite some time. Nobody took much notice at first. They just walked by on the other side, so to speak.'

'Yes, I know the story,' Matt said. 'Then what happened?'

'We get a lot of drunks, you know, Mr Stowe, but this one was special.' The waiter's eyes gleamed with eagerness as he spoke.

'In what way?'

'Ah, well, then the doc came by and looked at him and said, 'If we leave this man lying here, he's going to die from alcohol poisoning. So some of you boys raise him up and carry him into my office where I can pump him out.' So one or two of the boys did what the doc said.' A look of disappointment crossed the waiter's pale face. 'I don't know what happened after that. He might have passed on, so to speak.'

Matt walked to Doc Mason's office and went right in. He was confronted by Mrs Mason, a somewhat formidable woman, who stood in front of him to bar the door.

'The doctor's busy at the moment,' she said. 'Do you have some illness that needs treatment?'

'Good morning, Mrs Mason,' Matt said diplomatically. 'I believe a man was brought here earlier this morning, heavily drunk?'

'You believe right,' she said. 'But I think the man you mention is still undergoing treatment. He is very sick at the moment.'

'Then if you don't mind I'll just sit down and wait.'

Mrs Mason shrugged her shoulders and left him sitting in an overstuffed chair in the entrance hall.

He didn't have long to wait. After no more than a minute Doc Mason appeared, looking somewhat harassed.

'Mr Stowe,' he said in some surprise, 'what can I do for you?'

'How's the patient?' Matt enquired.

Doc Mason looked at him closely. 'I can't discuss my patients with you, Mr Stowe, unless you're a close relative.'

'Is he going to live?' Matt asked directly. Doc Mason shrugged his shoulders.

'That depends,' he said. 'When a man has drunk more than a skinful it can be touch and go. Why are you so interested in this case?'

'I'm interested because he was riding my horse.'

'Is that so?' Doc Mason said suspiciously.

'That is so,' Matt said. 'The Abe Benjamin gang stole our horses a week or two back and this *hombre* comes riding into town on my horse. That is why I'm here.'

Doc Mason gave him a wry smile. 'Now listen here, Mr Stowe. I understand what you're saying to me, but right now my patient is in no state to see anyone. You see, he's struggling for his life.'

'Have you seen him before?' Matt asked him.

'I've seen him, but not officially. I understand he's a wandering cowboy. Takes work wherever he can get it.'

'Well, something must have happened to make him drink so much,' Matt said. 'Maybe he found a big inheritance and decided to celebrate.'

Doc Mason grunted and turned away.

'I'll be back later,' Matt said, 'when he's had time to recover or die.'

Doc Mason opened a door and disappeared without saying anything more.

Bell was loading up the buggy when Matt emerged from the doc's office.

'You took your time,' she said. 'I thought you'd got yourself lost or something.'

'Not lost,' he said. 'In fact, I'm just beginning to find myself.' He told her what had happened in the doctor's office.

'You think the man's set to die?' she asked.

'We're all set to die,' Matt told her. 'Some later and some sooner. The fact that this *hombre* was riding Sullivan means he got him from the Abe Benjamin gang by some means or other. If we can make this guy talk he might give us a lead on them.'

'So, what do you mean to do?'

Matt looked up and down Main Street and considered matters. 'I think we should take the groceries home, then I'll come back later to talk to the guy. That is, if he's survived the ordeal by booze.'

'What about Sullivan?' she asked.

'We take Sullivan home with us, of course. After all, he belongs to me and he deserves the best. He's a damned fine horse.'

She gave him an arch look. 'You know what happens to horse-thieves, Matt!'

He raised an eyebrow. 'Don't believe everything you hear, Bell.'

When they reached the homestead Joe and Bethany were reaping the hay harvest out on the pasture with May. The weather had been good and they had had a second harvest, but the crop was far from plentiful. When Matt and Bell rode out to join them they took a break and a draught of May's cheesy beer.

'You got the supplies?' May asked Bell.

'We got more than the supplies,' Bell said. 'Matt got his horse, Sullivan, back.'

That made Joe's eyes pop. 'You got the horse?' he said in amazement. 'How about my horse Sentinel?'

Matt told Joe what had happened and Joe's eyes popped even more.

'That means we might have a handle

on the Benjamin bunch,' he said.

The two girls looked concerned.

'So I guess you'll be leaving us,' May said regretfully.

'No, ma'am,' Matt said. 'We don't aim to leave. All we want is to get those horses back and bring those bank robbers to justice. That's all we want.'

'How do you mean to go about it?' May asked.

The brothers looked at one another.

'Well, first off,' Matt said, 'we ride into town first thing tomorrow morning and try to get a handle on the truth.'

'That's what we do,' Joe agreed.

Supper that evening was a sombre affair. The only one looking happy was Bethany; she kept glancing across at Joe and blushing.

When they were settling down to sleep in the barn later, Matt said to his brother, 'What's with you and Beth?'

Joe looked at him in the gloaming. 'Nothing to speak of,' he said, somewhat sheepishly. 'Why do you ask?'

'I saw the way she looked at you at

supper. I hope you weren't playing any of your tricks on that young woman.'

Joe was grinning. 'Tricks? Would I play tricks on a lady?'

'I think you'd play tricks on any woman if you had the chance.'

Joe was silent for a moment and Matt saw his head rocking back and forth as though he was making up his mind to confess to something.

'Well, all right,' Joe said. 'Our lips did happen to meet once or twice out there on the pasture.'

Matt paused to consider the matter. 'Is that all?' he said.

Joe gave a low laugh. 'Not much more. We were too busy.'

'I hope you know what you're doing,' Matt said.

'Oh, I know.' Another pause. 'As a matter of fact, I've come to a decision.'

'A decision?'

'I think I'm going to ask that girl to marry me.'

'You *think* you're going to?'

'No, I'm going to; that's for sure.'

★　★　★

Shortly after sunup the two brothers set out for Dodge City. Matt was riding Sullivan, who had perked up wonderfully since Matt had reclaimed him, and Joe was riding one of the Inkpen horses. Before they mounted up Bethany ran out with a package of lunch for the two boys, but her obvious target was Joe, who accepted the package graciously.

Bell looked up at Matt and gave him a wink.

May stood aside and observed.

'Now, don't get yourselves into any kind of trouble,' she said, looking at Matt. Matt tipped his Stetson.

'Don't you worry, Mrs Inkpen,' he said.

The brothers headed straight for Doc Mason's place. They tied their horses to the hitching-rail and approached the door. This time Doc Mason himself answered.

'You're early,' he said, as though he had been expecting them.

'The early bird . . . ' Matt said. 'How's the worm doing?'

Doc Mason indulged him with a sceptical grin.

'The patient survived,' he said. 'He's sitting out at the back, trying not to attract too much attention. And right now he's got a very bad ache in the head which is likely to last all day and probably all day tomorrow too. And I'm a little busy at the moment. I'm about to pull an aching tooth or two.'

'If you don't mind, we'll just walk through and wish him good day,' Matt said.

The doc shook his head. 'Now don't go killing him off after all I've done to keep him alive.'

'Why don't you go ahead and pull those teeth before the patient dies from the pain,' Joe replied. Then Mrs Mason appeared.

'You want me to show these young men through, Arthur?' she asked.

The doc nodded. 'But don't let them kill the patient.'

Mrs Mason led them through the house to an outside area where they saw a young man with a cold pack held against his head. He was sitting back in a semi-reclining chair with his eyes closed, looking as pale as a living ghost.

'You've got visitors,' Mrs Mason said, touching him gently on the shoulder.

'What!' The patient jolted forward and grimaced in agony. He looked at the two brothers with horror. 'Who the hell are you? What do you want?'

'One question at a time,' Matt said. 'I'm the guy whose horse you were riding when you were drunk as a loon yesterday morning.'

The patient groaned. 'I can't talk about it right now. I'm sick. Can't you see that?'

Joe leaned over him and said: 'You look like a living corpse. That's what you look like.'

'And what we want is for you tell us why you were riding a stolen horse,' Matt added. The patient waved his hand.

'Leave me alone, won't you? Or help me on to my feet. I'm gonna throw up at any moment.'

'That's good,' Joe said. 'It'll make you feel a whole lot better.'

They hauled him to his feet and he lumbered off into the bushes to be violently sick.

'We'll be back later,' Joe called after him. 'What do we do now?' he said to Matt.

'Like you said, we'll be back later,' Matt replied. The two brothers walked away.

'Not too refreshing for the doc's garden,' Joe said as they untethered their horses and rode down to the Long Branch saloon.

In the saloon it was quiet except for the perennial poker players at the long table, who might have been there all night. The blowsy woman with the glittering trinkets whom they had seen the first time they were in the establishment was sitting with several other calico queens at a little table slightly apart, but the over-obsequious waiter was nowhere to be seen. Joe was staring at the table with the calico queens.

'Those floozies are looking a bit green round the girls this morning,' he said.

'Not as green as the doc's patient,' Matt replied. 'And it might be a good idea if you kept your eyes off them now you're kind of promised to Bethany.'

They went over to the bar and perched on a couple of stools.

'What will it be?' the bartender asked.

They ordered beers.

They were sitting at the bar, each meditating on his future when the swing doors were pushed open and three waddies came into the saloon, laughing and shouting at one another so loudly the whole place seemed to wake up with a start. The waddies were dressed in cowpoke outfits like they had just come off the range: chaps, leather vests, high dusty hats and leather riding gloves.

They swaggered over to the bar and

perched themselves on stools not far from the brothers.

'Did you ever see those guys before?' Joe muttered to Matt.

'I don't believe I ever did,' Matt said.

The leader of the bunch looked along the bar straight at them. 'Did you say something?' he said.

'Nothing for your ears,' Joe replied. 'We were just discussing the weather, if it's any of your business.'

'Any of my business,' the man said. 'What do you know about business, a fresh faced runt like you?'

His companions guffawed and threw back some of the whiskey they had ordered. Matt turned to Joe.

'Don't sass,' he said quietly. 'No point in getting roughed up by these cowboys.'

Though he spoke quietly, the noisiest of the bunch turned to them again.

'Something on your mind?' he asked, so loudly that even the poker players and the calico queens stared in their direction, wondering what was about to happen.

'We're just discussing private matters,' Matt said.

'Like what?' the man demanded, leaning heavily towards them.

'Like, it has nothing to do with you,' Joe piped up again.

A look like a thundercloud appeared on the man's face. Matt saw, in a moment, two things. First, the man's face was so pockmarked it looked like the craters of the moon. Second, for some reason the *hombre* was in an ugly mood and he was looking for someone to take it out on.

What do we do? Matt wondered. *Do we make some kind of cringing apology, or do we face up to the guy?*

The next second, the man had slid off his perch and was ambling towards them, looking none too friendly. His two companions had also quaffed back their whiskeys and left their perches.

'You want to apologize?' the pockmarked *hombre* asked in a voice like the crack of doom.

'What for?' Joe asked.

'For shooting off your mouth without respect,' the man growled.

The brothers exchanged glances and Matt nodded.

'Why, you young puppy dogs,' the man said. 'I've a good mind to grab you by the neck and bang your empty heads together.'

That might not be an empty threat, Matt thought as he stepped away from Joe to give them space. It was like David and Goliath, except that there were three Goliaths and two Davids, and no pebbles in the brook.

Now the pockmarked guy reached out suddenly and made a grab at Joe, He was surprisingly fast but Joe was faster. He dodged away as quick as a bird and grabbed at the bar. The next instant he had a bottle in his hand. But before he could use it to any effect, Matt came in sideways at the man and smashed his fists into his paunch. The man grunted and stepped back.

'Why, you poisonous runt!' he gasped. 'I'm gonna break you in two like your

164

mother won't recognize you!' He took a step towards Matt and made a swipe at him with his long arm . . . and missed!

Joe wasn't for wasting his breath: he brought the bottle down on the side of the man's head. It landed with a pulpy thud and knocked his Stetson askew.

The man reeled away and floundered against the bar.

His two companions had stopped laughing. They stood slightly apart with their hands on the butts of their guns.

'Don't even think about it,' a voice commanded. The bartender was standing behind the bar, pointing a shotgun in their direction.

'You insult a man, you have to pay,' one of the *hombres* growled.

'Not in here, you don't,' the bartender said. 'You want to settle matters you go right out on to Main Street and fight it out, but you're not gonna do it in here.'

The guy with the pitted face shook his head and readjusted his hat.

'You boys come outside if you've got

the guts and we'll finish it out there.' He was still aggressive but he sounded slightly shaken after the bang on his head.

'You go jump in the river,' Joe said.

The man with the pockmarked face scowled at Joe for a moment, then drew back.

'Come on, boys,' he said. 'Let's get out of this ornery dump. It stinks to high heaven, anyway.' He narrowed his eyes and looked directly at the brothers. 'You boys step outside and we'll be waiting for you.'

'Yeah, we'll be waiting,' the others echoed. 'You step outside you're nothing but meat for the dogs.'

The three cowpokes turned and ambled towards the door. The leader swung round at the entrance. 'We'll be waiting, you yellow-bellied cowards,' he said.

Matt turned to the barman. 'Thanks,' he said.

'Don't mention it,' the barman replied. He laid the shotgun on the bar. 'You were lucky, that time. We don't like bloodshed in here, so we have to be ready for anything.'

'You ever see those waddies before?' Matt asked.

'Oh, I know them,' the bartender said. 'They have a habit of threatening anyone they take a disliking to.'

The poker players were looking in their direction and so were the calico queens. The woman with the frills and furbelows got up from her table and approached the brothers.

'Mighty brave of you,' she said. 'You work real well together.'

'Thanks for the praise,' Joe said sarcastically.

'You aim to go out and fight them?' she purred.

'I think the party's over for the time being,' Matt told her.

'Well, as long as you're here we're at your service,' she said with an arch look and a flounce. The other girls giggled. The bartender was leaning forward on the bar.

'You boys got off lightly there,' he

said. 'The Hammer was all set to smash you to pieces.'

'Is that what they call the ugly guy?' Matt asked.

'Oh, yes, he's Hammer Macvey,' the bartender said. 'We know him well. Hammer never forgets and never forgives. So if you go out there you'd better look out for yourselves.'

'Who does he work for?' Joe asked him.

'Those boys do pretty well,' the bartender said. 'I believe they belong to the Ned Shanklin outfit.'

'Come again?' Matt said.

'Ned Shanklin,' the bartender said. 'He's a big cattle man around here. Drops in for refreshments from time to time.'

The brothers looked at one another and grinned.

★   ★   ★

'Time we talked to the patient again,' Matt said.

168

'Time we did,' Joe agreed.

They finished their beers and slid off their stools.

'Take care,' the bartender said. 'You go out there, it's likely the Hammer will still be waiting.'

'That's a chance we have to take,' Matt said.

The brothers moved to the door and checked their Colt Frontiers. Then they pushed back the doors, looked across Main Street, then right and left, but there was no sign of the cowpokes. In fact, since they had entered the Long Branch saloon traffic on the street had increased significantly and there were buggies and buckboards passing quite rapidly in both directions. But the street appeared to be clear of the cowpokes.

'Those guys were probably just letting out air,' Joe said. Matt was less confident.

'They're probably still around,' he said. 'I guess they went into another saloon to roust around.'

They unhitched their horses and

rode back down Main Street to Doc Mason's place. The doc was out on the sidewalk, looking somewhat anxious.

'If you boys came back to talk to that over boozed cowboy you're in for a disappointment,' he said, 'because the over boozed cowboy isn't here. He cut loose no more than half an hour back.'

'Is that so?' Joe said. 'You got any idea where he went?'

'It's more a question of why he went,' the doc replied. 'He just looked out and saw some people he recognized and he didn't like what he saw. In fact, I would say he was more than a little nervous.'

'So we lost our man,' Joe said, as they rode away from the doc's place.

Matt shook his head. 'I've got a hunch.'

'What sort of hunch?'

'A hunch that says we should look in at the sheriff's office.'

They rode on to the sheriff's office and hitched their horses to the rail. Then they went inside. The first thing they saw was Sheriff Luke Potter in his bowler. He was sitting behind his desk with a Colt .45 in front of him. Opposite, trying to look inconspicuous, was the drunk who had been riding Matt's horse. As they entered, he rose apprehensively, then sank back again. He was still yellow around the gills but not quite as yellow as before and his eyes were not quite as lustreless.

'You!' he said. 'What do you want with me?'

'Not much,' Matt replied. 'But it seems my hunch was right. I thought we might find you here.'

Potter was smiling. 'You've got a long nose, Mr Stowe,' he said.

'I know a rat when I smell one,' Matt replied. He looked at the man sitting opposite the sheriff and saw that he was scared out of his mind. 'So you've thrown yourself on the protection of the law?' he said.

Joe looked at the single-action Colt lying on the desk. 'You expecting trouble, Sheriff?'

Luke Potter was still grinning. 'An

officer of the law always expects trouble, Mr Stowe.'

Matt looked at the horse-thief again. 'Mind if I ask you one or two questions, mister?'

'Ask away,' the man said somewhat apprehensively.

The sheriff nodded and said nothing.

Matt drew up a chair and sat astride it with his elbows resting against the back.

'First off, do you ride with Ned Shanklin?'

The man nodded. 'I rode with him until a week back. Then I had to leave.'

'You had to leave?'

'There was an argument. I left because I knew they were out to get me.'

Matt looked at Luke Potter and Potter raised a cautious eyebrow.

'So that's why you're here?' Matt said. The man squirmed a bit in his chair.

'I'm here because I saw Hammer Macvey and I knew Shanklin had sent him to get me. Hammer isn't called Hammer for nothing. He's a rough customer and Shanklin sent him with two of the other boys.'

'The next question,' Matt said, 'is how did you come by my horse Sullivan?'

The man paused and his eyes darted round the room like a frightened bird looking for some way of escape.

'I'm going to make a suggestion,' Matt continued relentlessly. 'I suggest you got Sullivan from Abe Benjamin and his gang. Would that be right?'

Luke Potter's lips parted with astonishment. 'That would be right, Mr Stowe,' he agreed.

Matt sucked his lip. 'So, what you're telling me is that there's a tie up between Shanklin and Benjamin. Would that be right too?'

The man nodded. Then he looked at the sheriff.

'I'm no bad man, Sheriff. I just want to stay alive.'

'You've done the right thing,' Luke Potter said, looking somewhat triumphant.

7

The interview came to a sudden end when they heard the sound of gunfire outside. Sheriff Potter grabbed his Colt and sprang up from behind his desk. The man Matt had been questioning crouched behind the desk, as though trying to make himself invisible.

'That's them! They're coming to get me,' he cried.

Matt and Joe drew and cocked their Colt Frontiers.

They peered through the window and saw Hammer Macvey and his two buddies whirling round on horseback and firing their guns every which way. The people out on the street where scuttling into doorways or taking cover wherever they could.

'Give me a gun,' the drunk shouted. 'Give me a gun so I can protect myself.

I want to shoot that Hammer before he comes for me.'

'Don't go out there, Sheriff,' Matt advised. 'Those skookums are hungry for blood!'

Joe made a move for the door but Matt reached out and grabbed him by the arm.

'Not now!' he said. 'Keep it for later.'

'They're not coming this way,' Luke Potter said. 'I think they're riding out of town.' He watched as the three riders disappeared towards the outskirts of town in a cloud of dust. 'I better go over and see what's doing over there.'

He flung open the door and ran, head down, across Main Street towards the Crystal saloon.

Matt and Joe followed closely with their guns drawn. A man was standing aghast on the sidewalk with a hand pressed against his left shoulder.

'My gawd!' he shouted, 'they got me in the shoulder.'

'Go get Doc Mason,' Luke Potter told someone. But the doc was already on the scene. He examined the man's shoulder and said:

'Take him to my office. I'll be down there in less than a minute.'

They made their way into the saloon with their guns drawn. Inside there was a general panic and several people were gaping at the body of a man lying supine close to the bar. The doc knelt down beside him and examined him closely.

'I'm afraid he's gone,' he pronounced solemnly after a moment.

'Poor old Hank,' a woman wailed. 'He never did nobody any harm.'

'What happened?' Potter asked.

The bartender shook his head. 'That pockmarked *hombre* was out for blood. He just wanted to kill someone and it might have been anyone. Hank just stood up for himself and the man shot him down like he was nothing.'

'That might have been us,' Joe said quietly to Matt. 'What do we do: ride after those killers?'

'What we do is use our heads,' Matt replied.

They walked out, looked across Main Street and saw the drunk they had been questioning standing beside Matt's horse Sullivan with his hand on the bridle.

'Don't even think about it,' Matt shouted.

The man turned towards him. 'I wasn't going to go anywhere,' he said. 'I just want to help to catch those killers, that's all.'

'Well, we can help you there,' Matt told him. He walked right up to the man and held his gun against his chest. 'Why don't we just step inside the sheriff's office and talk things through?' Matt spoke in a quiet and even tone but there was no room for misunderstanding.

The man nodded and they went into the sheriff's office.

'First of all,' Luke Potter said to the brothers, 'If you're going to work with me I think I should deputize you two boys.' As usual, Matt and Joe exchanged glances.

'I don't think we can do that,' Matt said.

'Like we're both obligated to help Mrs Inkpen on the farm,' Joe explained.

'And it's a busy time,' Matt added.

'Well, that's too bad,' the sheriff said, 'because I have a hunch I'm going to need you.'

'Well, I have a hunch too,' Matt said.

'What's that, Mr Stowe?'

'I think we should talk a little more to that horse-thief in there.'

The man they had referred to as horse-thief was sitting on a bunk in one of the cells, probably meditating on his uncertain future.

Potter said: 'These gentlemen have a few more questions to ask you.'

The man got up from the bunk and came through to the main office. Potter gestured for him to sit down and he sat in the rush chair provided, looking straight across at Matt, who had his hands on the table and was staring at him. There was no doubt about who was to be the main questioner.

'Let's get down to business,' Matt said.

The man looked relieved. 'I want to help all I can, Mr Stowe.'

Matt nodded. 'First off, what's your name?'

'Miles Massingham. They call me Milo.'

'OK, Milo. Tell me something: what's the tie-up between the Benjamin bunch and Ned Shanklin?'

'They work together. Benjamin and his boys ride for Shanklin when the need arises.'

'You mean when there's cattle rustling to be done?'

'Well, that's right, Mr Stowe. And then, when there's no rustling, the Benjamin boys do thieving, like robbing banks and stuff like that.'

'So, how did you come to be in procession of my horse Sullivan?'

Milo looked away and then glanced in the direction of Matt again.

'I had difficulties with Mr Shanklin, so I decided to make a break. So I took the best horse I could find.'

'And the saddle to go with it?' Matt suggested.

Milo nodded in agreement. 'That was a fine tooled saddle. Shanklin refused to give me the money he owed me. So I took the horse and saddle and just made a run for it.'

'What about the booze? How come you almost drank yourself to death?'

Milo looked somewhat abashed. 'I took that in lieu of what was owed to me and just kept drinking until I was in a daze. I don't know how I got to Dodge City but that horse Sullivan has a lot of savvy and I guess he saved my life.'

'He's a damned fine horse,' Matt said. 'The next question is, can you lead us to the Shanklin spread?'

Milo's eyes darted all round the room in fear. 'That would be difficult, Mr Stowe. You saw what Hammer did to that poor soul over there. He would have done the same to me if he could have found me. That's what Shanklin sent him for.'

Matt sat back in his chair and spread

his hands. Sheriff Luke Potter gave a somewhat smug grin.

'Shanklin and Benjamin, two birds with one stone,' he said.

'Those birds have awful sharp claws,' Matt rejoined.

Potter nodded. 'Did you ever think about studying the law, Mr Stowe?'

'I thought about it once or twice,' Matt replied.

★   ★   ★

The brothers returned to the farm quite late that evening.

'So you're back!' May said in some surprise.

The young women looked on and said nothing.

'We brought supplies,' Joe said. 'Flour and a heap of beans and a few sweet potatoes. Paid on account.'

'Paid on account?' May said.

'Just so you'll know we mean to stay.' Joe smiled at Bethany and she blushed to the roots of her hair.

Bell gave Matt a cryptic look.

Joe then gave an account of all that had happened in Dodge City, with elaborate ornamentation. He liked telling stories and he thought he was good at it.

'You mean they shot Hank?' May said. 'Poor man! That's terrible.'

'We saw him lying there dead as a stuffed owl,' Joe said somewhat tactlessly.

'So, what's going to happen now?' May asked.

'Well, Mrs Inkpen,' Matt said, 'there's a big reward out for Benjamin and his bunch and our recent boss, Mr Calloway of the Snake spread, sent us on a reconnaissance mission.'

'What's a mission?' Bethany asked innocently.

'A mission is when someone sends you out to do something,' May informed her.

'My!' Bethany said. 'That sounds real important.'

Joe puffed himself up. 'He wanted us to look around in Dodge City and find out all we could about Ned Shanklin and what he does with those rustled cattle and where he trades them on.'

'Oh, my!' Bethany exclaimed. 'Like you're trying to track down on the rustlers?'

'That's right, Miss Bethany,' Matt said. 'And now we know there's a tie-up between Shanklin and the Benjamin gang.'

'Well, isn't that something!' Bethany exclaimed.

May Inkpen was looking at Matt. 'So what's your next move?' she asked.

Matt and Joe were silent for a moment. Though Joe enjoyed talking, when it was a matter of thinking and explaining, he usually left it to his brother.

Matt creased his brows. 'What we aim to do,' he said, 'is we're going to claim that reward on the Benjamin bunch and crack the rustling business at the same time.'

'That will be dangerous,' Bell said, shaking her head. 'How do you know you can trust that man Milo?'

'We don't exactly trust him,' Matt said, 'but we think we can rely on him to show us where Shanklin is holed up.'

'So, when will you leave?' May asked him. Joe looked at Matt.

'Tomorrow come sunup,' Matt said.

The brothers were going to pick Milo up from the sheriff's office in Dodge City early next morning, so it was time to hit the hay: quite literally, since they were still sleeping in the barn.

But the brothers were restless and Joe said he wanted a few moments alone with Bethany. So he wandered off into the darkness for their assignation.

Matt walked down to the pasture and looked across the plains towards Dodge City, where he could see lights twinkling. Just like the stars had dropped to earth, he thought. But then he heard a rustling sound quite close by and he turned to see the form of a woman. She came quickly to his side.

'So you haven't settled to sleep yet?' she asked.

'Not yet,' he said. 'I was feeling kind

of restless and now I look at those stars up there they seem to be telling me something.'

'Maybe they're trying to talk sense into you, Mr Stowe,' she said, and he could tell by her voice that she was smiling.

'What does that mean?' he asked. She was so close now he could see her breath in the air.

'I think they say. 'Don't be a damned fool, Matt Stowe'.'

'Is that a fact, Miss Bell?' He laughed. 'Why do they say that?'

She breathed in slowly. 'They think your mission is very dangerous, Matt Stowe, and you shouldn't be doing it.'

There was a pause. Then he reached out impulsively and took her hand.

'Is that what you think too?' he murmured.

Now they were standing so close together he could see her eyes shining.

'That's what I think too,' she said. 'But I know why you're doing it and I want to come with you.'

Now Matt's arm encircled her waist and it seemed the most natural thing in the world.

'You can't come, Miss Bell, and you know it, but I have a better idea.'

'What's that, Mr Stowe?'

They stood for a moment and then he felt her cheek burning against his.

'What you do, Miss Bell, is you wait for me here and give me a promise that will carry me through.'

'What promise is that, Mr Stowe?' she murmured.

He waited for a moment, then said close to her ear: 'Promise that when I get back you will marry me.'

There was a breathless pause.

'I promise,' she whispered.

They stood for a long time, their cheeks warm and burning, and then they kissed.

* * *

The brothers rode out towards Dodge City at dawn. Both had slept quite peacefully. May had prepared enough food for several days and, despite the early hour, she and the girls were up to see them off.

Everything lay in deceptive peace as they rode into the town that called itself a city.

'I'm riding with you,' Luke Potter announced when they got there. He looked like a different person. He had changed into range clothes and discarded his bowler in favour of a floppy hat. 'I've appointed one of my deputies to look after the place while I'm gone.'

Milo was tending the horses but, even in the early light, he seemed a little nervous. He was wearing a gunbelt with a revolver that Luke Potter had lent him.

'Just as long as I don't fall into the hands of that Hammer, I'll be OK,' he said.

Matt wasn't convinced. 'All we want is for you to show us where Shanklin holes up,' he said. 'Then we'll decide on our next move.'

'That's all right by me,' Milo said. 'Gunplay isn't my bag.'

'And don't bring any dumb-brained whiskey for the journey,' Matt told him.

Before they could mount up, a man ran across the street with a paper in his hand.

'Sheriff!' he cried, 'I've just got news through. There's been another bank robbery.'

Luke Potter leaned over, took the paper and read it. Then he looked at Matt.

'Small bank in a town east of here, called Clintock. They hit it last night just before closing time. It says there were four of them and it sounds like the Benjamin bunch. It doesn't mention injuries or deaths. It just says they got away with a whole bag of money.'

Milo had been listening intently. 'Why Clintock?' he said. 'That's not far from the the Ned Shanklin spread.'

'Looks like we're on the right track,' Potter said. 'Let's go, boys.'

They rode out of town towards the

east. Potter was in the lead with Milo, who was doing his best to look like an army scout.

'You reckon we're doing the right thing here?' Joe asked his brother.

'You mean you don't think much of the company?' Matt suggested.

Joe shook his head. 'Well, I'm wondering, Matt. Maybe we should have gone back and made our report to Calloway. I think he deserves to be in on this.'

Matt rode on thoughtfully. 'You got a point there,' he admitted after a minute or two. 'But maybe we should just look the place over, see if we can trust this Milo guy. There's something about him that smells a little unwholesome to me.'

'You mean like bad?'

Matt nodded. 'I think you got it. And another thing. This Luke Potter character. Now he's wearing range clothes he looks like an actor pretending to be what he isn't. I think I prefer the dark suit and the bowler hat. That seems more like his true nature.'

That was a long speech for Matt but Joe could see what he meant: a man who changes hats is like a man who sometimes wears a beard and sometimes shaves clean; he isn't quite sure who he is.

'Another thing,' Matt said. 'Calloway might not give a damn, one way or the other, about the Benjamin bunch.'

'You mean if we bring those boys to justice by ourselves, we get the reward. Is that what you're thinking?'

'I'm thinking about May Inkpen and those two girls,' Matt said. 'If we get the reward we might just help them to keep the farm and that's what the marshal would have wanted. Don't you think so?'

Joe grinned. 'I think that's a beautiful idea,' he said.

★ ★ ★

By nightfall they were still quite a long way from the Ned Shanklin spread according to Milo. So they scouted around for a suitable place and set up camp beside a tributary of the Arkansas River. Matt and Joe did most of the work. Matt selected the camp site and sent Milo and Potter out to gather kindling and Joe sorted through the supplies to rustle up a meal. When the fire was going well they gathered round and Joe took charge. They had watered the horses and hobbled them in a lush hollow close by the camp.

'It's gonna be mighty cold tonight,' Milo said nervously, edging close to the fire.

Luke Potter looked at him a little anxiously. 'You been doing ranch work long?' he asked Milo.

'Long enough,' Milo said. 'What I want is to go back East and find myself a little nest to rest up in.'

'You'll be lucky if you keep on drinking the way you did,' Potter advised.

Milo looked thoughtful. 'I think I've given up on that stuff,' he said. 'I hope to live to a ripe old age after we get ourselves clear of Ned Shanklin and his bunch.'

'Not to mention Benjamin,' Joe put in from the fire. Then he started doling out the supper on tin plates and handing it round. Nobody asked about the food; they just tucked in and washed it down with water from the creek.

'What about Shanklin?' Joe said.

'What about him?' Milo asked, looking right and left as though he thought the rustler might be edging up on them in the dusk.

'How many hands in his bunch?'

'Well, there's Hammer, of course, and about six more, not including the Benjamin boys. They drift in and out, but my guess is we're dealing with around ten.'

'Ten or more?' Luke Potter looked amazed.

'At least,' Milo said, looking away from the fire again.

Joe glanced at Matt. Matt elevated his eyebrows and raised his tin mug of coffee.

'Slainte!' he said.

Sunup again! It had been very cold during the night but, when Matt stirred himself the fire was already burning brightly and Joe was rustling up breakfast from the eggs and a little ham that May had provided.

Milo was still groaning under his blanket. Sheriff Luke Potter was sitting up and lighting a pipe he had produced from somewhere.

'Always start the day with a pipe,' he said to Matt. 'Puts me on form for the day and helps me to think.'

'Well, I'm glad of that because we're going to need a deal of thinking,' Matt replied.

After breakfast they smothered the fire and obliterated as much of the campsite as possible. Then they gathered the horses, mounted up and rode on, with Potter and Milo in the lead as before.

'You think we're on a fool's errand?' Joe asked his brother again.

'Like I said,' Matt replied. 'Luke Potter is none too reliable and Milo has an unhealthy smell about him. So maybe we are.'

But there wasn't time for further discussion since, as they topped a rise, Potter reined in his horse and held up his hand.

'Woah!' he said, like a cavalry officer bringing his troop to a halt. The brothers pulled up alongside him and looked out over the flat land beyond. Everything was glimmering with early sunshine.

'What do you see?' Joe asked.

'Riders,' Potter told him. 'Down there about a mile ahead. I count three.'

Matt drew out the small telescope he always carried and trained it on the riders. As Potter had said, there were three.

'Let me take a looksee,' Milo said. Matt handed him the telescope.

'Yes, I see them, and that big guy is Hammer Macvey unless I'm a jackass.'

Nobody contradicted him. Then Joe took a look.

'Yes, that's Hammer,' he said. It was the three waddies who had confronted them at the Long Branch and had later killed old Hank in the Crystal saloon.

'So, we caught up on them,' the sheriff said with some satisfaction.

'Not yet,' Matt replied cautiously. 'Now we have to catch them in the net.'

'Four to three. It should be easy,' Potter said.

'Nothing's easy where Hammer's concerned,' Milo warned.

'What do we do now?' Joe asked.

Matt pointed below and to the right. 'We know where they're headed. I think we should ride along that draw. That way they won't see us.'

'Seems like a good move,' Potter said. 'Maybe you should have been a general and not a lawyer after all.'

'I know that draw,' Milo piped up. 'I've pushed beef along it many times.'

Matt scanned the waddies through his telescope again.

'Those boys must have gone that way themselves,' he said. 'So maybe it isn't

195

such a good idea, after all.'

'Best way to go, whichever way you look at it,' Potter said. 'If we ride straight along through the creosote and scrub we'll be right out in the open and easy to pick out.'

Matt could see the point of that, though he felt a little uneasy about the tactic.

'Just as long as you realize there's going to be gunplay here,' he reminded them.

'One way or the other, we've got to take them in, dead or alive,' Potter said.

'As far as Hammer's concerned, I prefer him dead,' Milo replied.

As they rode on down the draw, which had obviously been used many times before to drive cattle, Matt felt less and less like a general and more and more like a damned fool. *If I were a general*, he thought, *I'd be a lot more cautious*. He was reminded of Custer and his last stand where the lives of about two hundred and fifteen troopers had been thrown away needlessly at the greasy grass just because of one man's arrogance.

'I don't think we should bunch up, Sheriff,' he said. 'I think I should scout ahead.'

'I don't like that,' Joe protested. 'If you want to go ahead, I'm gonna ride with you.'

'I can't let you do that,' Matt said. 'Think of that girl Bethany. She's waiting for you'

'Well, I'll be giving you cover all the way,' Joe promised.

Matt scanned the rocks to right and left as he rode. *I'm not going to die like Custer*, he said to himself. *I'm going to keep cool and ride right on through this draw to the other end.* In fact, he had almost reached the other end when what he had feared actually occurred. Some say that you don't hear the one that hits you but that isn't true. The one that hit Matt took his Stetson right off and spun it to the ground. By good fortune, the bushwhacker had aimed a couple of inches too high.

An instant later Matt plunged from his horse's back and dived for the scrub. I have been a damned fool, he thought. He looked back along the trail and saw the others dismounting and diving for cover. Joe rose from behind a boulder and started crawling towards him. Then another shot rang out and Joe ducked down behind a rock.

'Keep your head down,' Matt shouted. 'I'm OK.'

There was a moment of silence, then there came a kind of scrabbling sound from above on the left. *Maybe there's more than one of them*, he thought.

He looked up and waited, but not for long. There was a flash from above and he managed to pinpoint it. Then, taking a chance while the bushwhacker reloaded his Springfield, he leaped from cover and pulled Sullivan round behind a larger bush. Then he yanked out his Winchester and levered it. *He's up there just to the left of that rocky outcrop*, he said to himself. He levelled the Winchester and waited. Someone up there was moving from rock to rock for cover. Whoever he was he was no fool.

There was another flash and the bullet sprayed chips from the rock quite close to his head — a damned sight too close for comfort. He looked back and saw Joe crawling towards him from cover to cover. He waited as Joe crawled right up to him.

'I told you to keep your head down!' he said.

'What's the plan?' Joe asked hopefully.

Matt gave a low chuckle; if only it was just a matter of making a plan!

'Listen,' he said. 'Those cowboys must have known we were tailing them. Maybe they even saw our fire last night. So they decided to lure us into a trap. I was a damn fool to suggest following them down this draw. That's exactly what they were hoping for.'

'Then what do we do?' Joe asked.

Matt considered the matter. 'What would they expect us to do?'

Joe thought for a moment. 'They

probably think we'll turn tail and run.'

'Well,' Matt said, 'I think you might be right at that. Which means we have to do something different.'

'Like what?'

'Like I make my way up there and you give me as much cover as possible.'

Joe shook his head. 'That's not a good plan. You get up there, they'll be waiting for you.'

'There are more ways to trap a coyote than one.' Matt said. 'Like they can see us from up there, but if I crawl up through that chimney I'll be out of sight unless they lean right out to look. That's when you can put a bullet in them.'

Joe took time to think: perhaps too long. The bushwhacker fired another shot: it was the Springfield again, a little too close for comfort. The horse Joe had been riding screamed, reared right up and fell, jerking on to its side.

They heard a mocking laugh from above.

'Well, that means retreating's gonna

be difficult,' Joe said aghast. 'Poor beast.'

'And another thing,' Matt said. 'That means this is where the action will be. They don't want us to retreat.'

'So it's back to your plan,' Joe said. Matt patted him on the arm.

'OK, I'm on my way. Keep me covered as much as you can.'

He slithered out from behind the boulder and started to worm his way through the scrub towards the chimney-like hollow he had indicated. As he slid and crawled he could hear an exchange between Luke Potter and Milo. He could tell by Milo's tone that he wanted to pull out and retreat by the way they had come. His voice sounded like that of a whining cat.

'You down there, Milo?' a voice called from above. 'You yellow-bellied skunk. Why don't you just get on your horse and ride back the way you came? Make me a good target.'

A man who is talking and laughing is a sonofabitch who can't concentrate on his shooting, Matt thought as he crawled his way to the chimney. The bushwhacker had said *make me a good target*. That might mean he was on his own. But you can't be too careful.

Matt was now at the bottom of the chimney. He looked up and plotted his way. The chimney was quite steep but there were small outcrops and ledges and handholds: he reckoned he could hoist himself up without too much trouble. Pushing the Winchester ahead would be difficult but he still had his Colt Frontier if needs be. If he got to the top, he figured, it would bring him to within a yard or two from the bush-whacker to the bushwhacker's right, unless the bushwhacker moved on.

Climbing up that chimney seemed to take an eternity and he paused from time to time to catch his breath. Fortunately, the hombre above had started a shouting match with his intended victims.

'I got you in my sights, Milo boy,' the man shouted. 'Why don't you just throw that gun down and come crawling out with your hands up? I might even spare your miserable life at that!' Matt didn't recognize the voice but he reckoned it wasn't Hammer Macvey's.

'OK, you've had your fun,' another voice retorted from below; it was Luke Potter talking. 'You know you killed a harmless man back there in Dodge and there's a price on your head.'

'Not me,' the voice replied. 'I'm no man-killer. I just shoot down rats like you.' He fired off another round, this time in the direction of Luke Potter and Milo.

Matt was glad of the altercation. It kept the bushwhacker busy and it also gave him time to climb without being heard. It also confirmed his suspicions: there was probably only one bushwhacker and it wasn't Hammer Macvey. He was almost at the top of the chimney and he leaned out just far enough to see Joe, who was staring up from behind the boulder, wondering how he was doing. Matt gave a signal that said: *I'm going in now.*

Joe fired a shot in the direction of the bushwhacker, who laughed.

'Better luck next time, sonny,' he shouted.

Now Matt was at the top of the chimney, where it opened out. Above him he saw sage bushes and other shrubs and beyond them, almost to his surprise, he saw the bushwhacker in profile. It wasn't Hammer Macvey: it was one of his partners.

Matt knew he couldn't level his Winchester. So he reached down, drew his Colt Frontier and levelled it at the waddy.

'Just drop that gun and throw up your hands,' he called.

A look of astonishment appeared suddenly on the man's face. He whirled round with the Springfield but it was too late. Then Matt, as he jerked the trigger of his Colt, started to slide backwards and the shot went wide. The man started towards him, but it was too late to reload the Springfield — too late for anything much at all. The crack of a

Winchester echoed in the gully. The waddy jerked back with a look of amazement on his face, and fell.

Matt scrambled out of the chimney with his Colt levelled. As he approached the fallen man the waddy looked up at him, gasped, 'I'm killed!' as though he didn't believe it, then fell back and died.

8

'That's Al Benito,' Milo said, looking down at the dead man's face.

Matt knew that already. Benito had been with Hammer when Hammer Macvey had picked a quarrel with the brothers in the Long Branch saloon. Now, as he lay dead, he still looked somewhat surprised and aggrieved. *That's no way to go!* Matt thought, not for the first time.

'What do we do now?' Milo asked Matt. 'Do we leave him here for the buzzards and the coyotes?'

'The buzzards won't mind,' Matt said, 'as long as they get their gutful.'

After the gunfight Milo had climbed up through the chimney as nimbly as a cat. Now he and Matt scrambled down again to join the other two. Matt looked at Joe and nodded.

'Thanks,' he said quietly. 'I think you

probably saved my hide.'

Joe nodded. He wasn't used to compliments, especially from his brother.

Luke Potter joined them and the four of them squatted down together in a sheltered spot.

'What do we do now?' Milo asked.

Luke Potter looked at Matt thoughtfully. 'Ask the general,' he said with a tinge of irony.

Matt considered matters. It was a big responsibility.

'Well,' he said, after a moment, 'they obviously know we're on our way. In fact they knew we were coming down the draw. That means the element of surprise is lost even if we had it in the first place. So, riding on down the draw, we might be sticking our heads in a noose.'

There was a pause.

'I think we have to go back the way we came,' Potter said. 'Live to fight another day.'

'Only one thing,' Joe pointed out. 'We might be in a trap both ends.'

'What does that mean?' Milo asked.

'That means they might have boxed us in.'

'Like, some of those skookums rode back on the higher ground to cut us off, you mean?'

'But there were only three. Now there are just two,' Luke Potter said.

'Don't be fooled by that,' Matt put in. 'We saw three but there will be others. Like you said, Milo, Shanklin is in cahoots with Abe Benjamin, and Benjamin and his bunch, as we know only too well, are very ugly *hombres*.'

'What do you think about that, Milo?' Joe asked.

'That's a difficult question to answer,' Milo said. 'Shanklin is a hard man but he's a businessman too. Like, he sent Hammer out to get me but he doesn't care for competition. Probably reckons Benjamin's getting too big for his cowboy boots.'

Another pause.

'I think we go back,' Matt said. 'We have to hope they don't aim to give us to the buzzards.'

They rode back through the gully. Joe and Matt were mounted on Sullivan and Matt felt rather stupid.

'Those guys were playing with us,' he said quietly to his brother.

'We were damned fools to ride down this draw,' Joe muttered.

Once more Milo and Luke Potter were slightly ahead, spaced as much apart as possible. Luke Potter was leading the way, looking cautiously to left and right.

Matt felt like a sitting duck. Anybody gunning down on them from above could shoot the two brothers with one blast. If he could bring down Sullivan they might both be dead and cold.

But on this ride the gods favoured them and they emerged from the draw without incident.

Potter again held up his arm like a cavalry commander and they all drew rein.

'Well, gentlemen,' he said, 'I've come to a decision. This has been a wild-goose chase and I'm going back to Dodge City to keep the peace there.'

'Well, that's your choice, Sheriff,' Matt said. 'You go right ahead.'

'I think I'll come with you, Sheriff,' Milo announced.

'You do realize those *hombres* will be coming after you,' Joe told him.

Milo shrugged. 'I don't think so,' he said. 'Not where I'm going.'

'Then good luck to you,' Joe said.

'Just one thing,' Matt added. 'We need to know exactly where Ned Shanklin keeps his rustled cattle.'

Milo looked doubtful for a moment, then he brightened up.

'That's easy. I'll draw you a map.'

They dismounted to let the horses get their breath back. Milo got out a pencil and sketched a map on a grubby scrap of paper he took from his pocket.

'It's right here. You follow through towards the Arkansas River until you get to this butte, then you follow a stream until you come to this valley, and this' — he stabbed at the paper with his pencil — 'and this right here is where the ranch is. Just a small place but that's where he keeps the cattle. Shanklin doesn't keep them long, just long enough to rebrand them and ship them East at Wichita or Ellsworth, whichever suits him best.'

'Thanks for that.' Matt took the paper and stuffed it into his pocket.

★   ★   ★

Matt and Joe watched as Luke Potter and Milo rode away.

'What do we do now?' Joe asked his brother.

'Whatever we do, we're better off without those two knuckle heads,' Matt said. 'So what we do is we find a place to camp and have us a meal. Lucky you rescued the supplies from that poor dead horse of yours.'

'That was a bad business,' Joe said. 'That horse belonged to May Inkpen. She's not gonna be too happy about that.'

'That's a pity,' Matt said. 'Especially since she's your future mother-in-law . . . unless you change your mind.'

They found a sheltered place to camp and made themselves as comfortable as possible considering the circumstances. Matt built a fire and Joe did the cooking, which suited them both very well.

'What's the strategy?' Joe asked when they were settled by the fire.

Matt grinned at him. 'Good word that; you're growing up fast, boy.'

'I can't let you have all the best words,' Joe quipped. 'Just showing I do have a brain. It might be a bit small but I try to keep it active. So I'll ask again: what do you think we should do now?'

'Well, the way I see it we have three options,' Matt said. 'The first is we report back to base.'

'You mean go back to the girls?'

Matt grinned. 'The second is we ride back to the Snake outfit and show Calloway the map.'

'You mean like two puppy dogs bringing back a bone?' Joe said, impersonating a whining puppy. 'You said there were three options. What's the third?'

Matt moistened his lips and stared at his brother.

'We could ride on to Clintock. That's where the Benjamin bunch did their last bank job, remember?'

Joe did remember. He gave a whistle of surprise. The idea pleased him, though he wasn't sure why.

'What do we do there?' he asked.

'We look around and see what we can pick up,' Matt said. 'Be like a holiday for you,' he added with a wink.

Joe grinned but didn't wink back. He was thinking of Bethany Inkpen.

'What about the horse?' he asked.

'You got a point there,' Matt said, 'but I don't think Sullivan will mind too much. He's strong and broad-minded and we don't have to push him too hard.'

'Like, we ride into Clintock on one horse looking like two hick cowboys without a dime between us?'

'We did it before at Dodge,' Matt said.

'And look where it got us!' Joe exclaimed.

Matt shrugged. 'One thing leads to another. If we hadn't ridden into Dodge on that flea-bitten nag we wouldn't have met Marshal Inkpen and his wife and daughters, would we?'

Joe broke into a smile. 'You got a point there, Matt. So we ride on to Clintock and see where that takes us.'

*   *   *

Sullivan was indeed a valiant horse and the brothers treated him with the respect he deserved. On the morning of the third day they rode into Clintock. In fact, to avoid looking too much like greenhorns, Joe decided to dismount just outside the town limits and lead Sullivan in: he figured it looked a lot more dignified, one man leading another man into town on his horse.

Clintock was the nearest to a one-horse town that they could think of: just one store, a livery stable, a bank, and not much more. So they drew up outside the bank and Matt dismounted.

'You boys looking for something?' a woman's voice piped up.

'Is there a hotel in this town?' Joe asked her.

The woman gave him a strange look, as if he had just dropped in from the moon.

'We don't have no hotel,' she said. 'Why do you want a hotel? There's a saloon just along from here, The Howling Wolf. They sometimes have folks staying there.'

She scratched her scraggy head, looked them up and down and decided the seemed harmless enough.

'You could always stay at my place, just as long as it ain't too long. We sometimes accommodate strangers.'

'Well, thank you kindly, ma'am,' Joe said in his most ingratiating tone.

'You only got one horse between you?' the woman asked disdainfully.

'The other one died,' Joe said. 'Met with an accident along the way.'

The old woman sniffed. 'Well that's a mighty fine-looking horse. Why don't you bring him to the back of the house and my man will feed him up and give him a good long drink. He looks as thirsty as a beached whale.'

'Well, thank you, ma'am,' Joe said politely.

Matt led Sullivan to the back of the house where there was quite an ample barn with room for a dozen horses. In fact there were two grazing inside and they looked up and whinnied in greeting as Sullivan was led in.

What they might have described as an old geek appeared to greet them.

'Howdy!' he said.

The woman explained in a high shriek that the brothers had just ridden in and were seeking hospitality.

'You're welcome,' the old geek said, 'just as long as you got the money to pay.'

Joe looked at Matt and Matt nodded.

'We can pay,' he said, 'as long as it doesn't break the bank.'

'Speaking of banks,' the old lady said, 'we had a hold-up a few days ago. Did you hear about that?'

'We heard about it,' Matt said.

'Abe Benjamin and his gang,' Joe added somewhat indiscreetly.

The old man's eyes popped. 'You know Benjamin?' he squawked.

'We met him once,' Joe said. 'He and his bunch took our horses and most of what we possessed.'

'Those men are bad medicine,' the old woman said. 'Why don't you strip off your duds and get yourselves under the pump. Then I'll rustle up a meal for you. I daresay you can use one.'

'Sure can!' Joe said. 'I'm as hungry as a bear.'

'And twice as ugly,' the old geek quipped.

Some minutes later Joe was shivering in a stream of cold water under the pump.

'Like you said, Matt, one thing leads to another. Looks like we got lucky again. It's a cold as hell under here.'

Matt grunted. He would have pre-ferred a bath full of hot water but a cold shower did at least wash off most of the grime and sweat.

It turned out that the old woman, whose name was Charlotte Middleton, wasn't a bad cook. She served up a more than passable meal with beef and dump-lings and even a few greens and root vegetables, which pleased the brothers well. The old man, Wilbur, dished out some of his home-brewed beer, which had a kick like a mule.

The room they were shown into had a twangy double bed, though the straw-stuffed mattress left much to be desired.

'You think we can sleep here?' Joe asked.

'Best choice we have,' Matt said.

Though it was still early in the day they lay down side by side. Within less than a minute they were oblivious to the outside world.

★ ★ ★

Matt woke to the sound of a cock crowing. For a moment he couldn't remember where he was. Then he heard a snore from his brother; he shook his head. It was one of the few times he had woken before Joe, who was usually busy cooking breakfast by now when they were on the trail. Matt rolled off the bed and pulled on his boots. The next moment Joe was sitting up and blinking.

'Where the hell are we?' he asked.

'You're right here with me,' Matt said, 'and we're just about to have us some breakfast.'

'Well, I'll be damned!' Joe exclaimed as he pulled on his boots. 'D'you realize we slept through the whole night on top of this bed in our clothes? I don't even remember taking off my boots, you know that?'

'I know right enough. I pulled them off after you fell back and started to snore.'

They went down the creaky stairs, which led directly into the room below

219

where Charlotte Middleton was already busy at the table.

'Got your breakfast good and ready,' she said. 'Ham and eggs and coffee, as much as you want.'

'Well, thank you, ma'am,' Joe said.

Matt nodded. 'Thank you, ma'am.'

The old man came in and sat down at the table with them.

'You boys sleep well?' he asked. 'That home brew I give you tends to knock people out real cold.' He gave a hoarse squeaky laugh like the hinge of a rusty door. 'I hope you don't have a sore head. I should have warned you.' The rusty door hinge squeaked again. 'By the way, Sheriff Cole looked in last night. Said he'd like to talk to you boys.'

'I guess we'd like to talk to him too,' Joe replied. 'And no, we don't have sore heads.' He looked at Matt and winked.

★   ★   ★

Sheriff Cole was a belt-and-braces man. He had wide-strapped suspenders and a

220

wide brown belt to keep his trousers secure. He wasn't a full-time sheriff. He also ran the general store with his wife and daughter.

'So, you boys rode into town last noon?' he said.

'Yes, we did,' Matt said.

They introduced themselves.

'The brothers Stowe,' the sheriff said. 'My good friend Wilbur tells me you know Abe Benjamin. Would that be right?'

'We don't exactly know him. We met him recently when he and his bunch robbed us on the trail. Took our horses and left us with an old coon-footed nag.'

Cole's eyes twinkled with humour. 'I heard a lot more than that.'

'Well, it's probably not much more than a fable,' Joe said.

'Fable it might be,' Cole said. 'It tells me you boys rode out after the Benjamin bunch when they robbed the bank in Dodge and ex-marshal Steve Inkpen got himself killed.'

'He didn't exactly get himself killed,' Matt said. 'He died of a heart attack.'

'Well, whatever happened, he ended up dead.' Sheriff Cole grinned. 'Inkpen was a good man. Pity I couldn't get to the funeral. But that's by the way.' He looked at the brothers and seemed to size them up. 'You know there's a substantial reward out for those killers, don't you?'

'We did hear a rumour to that effect,' Matt said.

'And we aim to claim it,' Joe put in a little too enthusiastically.

Cole chuckled. He was a big man but his laugh was low and musical; Matt wondered whether he enjoyed singing.

'That's a big ambition,' Cole said with an edge of sarcasm. 'How do you mean to go about it?'

'Well, to begin with, we think we might know where he holes up,' Joe said with his usual indiscretion.

Cole raised his eyebrows and nodded. 'You think you know where he's at? How come?'

'Well, Sheriff, it's like this. A couple of days back we were bushwhacked in a draw not too far from here. Joe's horse was killed but we managed to shoot the bushwhacker before he could shoot us. We happen to know that the man who tried to kill us was a buddy of a man called Hammer Macvey.'

Cole's eyes narrowed. 'I've heard of Hammer Macvey. Works for a rancher name of Shanklin, I believe.'

'You believe right,' Matt said. 'But you might not know that Abe Benjamin works for Shanklin too, when he's not robbing banks. Not only that but Shanklin is a cattle-rustler. So the whole thing ties up rather neatly.'

Sheriff Cole looked impressed. 'How do you boys know all this?'

Joe looked at Matt and Matt told Cole the whole story, except for the map that Milo had drawn.

Cole was silent for almost a minute: Matt could hear a clock ticking menacingly from close by.

'So you really think you can locate those bank robbers?' the sheriff said at last.

'I believe we can,' Matt said.

'I'm sure we can,' Joe proclaimed, somewhat more optimistically. Again Cole paused.

'Well, there's only one thing we can do,' he said. 'We get a posse together and ride out after those monkeys. If you're telling the truth on this, you could be in line for that reward I mentioned.'

'I hope so,' Joe said. 'It's just what we need.'

Back in the Middleton place, the brothers sat at the table and discussed the situation.

'You didn't show him the map,' Joe said.

Matt agreed. 'I didn't show him the map because he might want to claim the reward himself and we need the money to help out May Inkpen and the girls.'

'Well, that's good thinking,' Joe said, 'just as long as we can rely on that map.'

Matt got out the scrap of paper with the sketch map on it and spread it on the table.

'How do we know the Benjamin bunch

went back to the Shanklin ranch?' Joe asked.

'We don't,' Matt said. 'But I have a hunch we'll be going in the right direction. I think Benjamin and Shanklin are so close that they might as well be twins.'

'I think you might be right on that, too,' Joe said in some surprise.

★   ★   ★

That evening Charlotte Middleton produced another sample of her excellent cooking and the two boys tucked into it with gusto.

'So, you boys are on the trail of those bank robbers?' Charlotte asked them directly.

'How d'you know that?' Joe asked her.

She smiled and placed her finger against the side of her right nostril. 'There ain't much in this town that goes by unknown,' she said. 'You boys rode into town last afternoon. We knew you had some business and you weren't selling sewing machines either.' She gave her usual high-pitched shriek of laughter. 'Another thing I guess is you don't have two beans to rub together between you. So I don't want you boys to worry yourselves about money. You can think of yourselves as our guests until you bring those desperadoes to book.'

'Well, that sure is generous,' Joe said somewhat over-gushingly.

Sheriff Cole and Mrs Cole and their daughter Ruby had been invited to share the supper. Wilbur Middleton had actually had a shave to mark the occasion. Mrs Cole was as good-humoured as her husband. She managed the store, which sold practically everything under the sun. Ruby was quite sociable but she didn't say much since she was eclipsed by her mother, who never missed a chance for a good gossip.

They all squeezed round the only table in the place and Meg Cole pronounced it cosy. It turned out that she and the sheriff had two grown boys as well as Ruby and both had moved East to attend college; the elder boy, Brad, was engaged to be married.

'Those boys are bettering themselves,' Cole said, 'and we're glad of it.'

As the Coles spoke of their family Ruby looked down modestly, but Matt could see from Joe's expression that he was impressed by her good looks and demure deportment.

Meg Cole confessed that she had met May Inkpen and thought she was 'a brave woman who knew her own mind'.

The sheriff was not only a belt-and-braces man, he also had a habit of speaking bluntly and to the point. At the end of the meal, he said:

'Well, boys, I've gathered a small posse together and we aim to leave come sunup to flush out those desperadoes.'

He looked at Matt. 'Are you with us?' He gave Matt a piercing but good-natured look.

Matt spoke without hesitation. 'That's what we're here for, sir.'

'Well, that's good,' the sheriff said. 'That's very good indeed.'

* * *

Come sunup next morning, a whole bunch of men assembled outside the sheriff's office. They were all armed with Winchesters of one vintage or another, and sidearms. Some had other guns and shotguns too. On the outside they looked like a formidable and determined bunch.

Sheriff Cole mounted his horse and swung round to address the men.

'Before we ride out, I want you to know something,' he said. 'This is a dangerous business and one or two of you might get hurt or even killed. I hope you realize that.'

'That's OK,' a man called Giles piped up. 'Just as long as we bring those bank robbers to justice, we'll be happy.'

The other members of the posse gave him a rousing cheer.

'We might be gone for a week or more. I want you to understand that too,' Cole said.

'We got our rations,' Giles said. 'In

fact we got everything we need.'

'Be good to get away from the nagging wife for a bit,' another man shouted.

Hoots of laughter from the men; cries of 'Shame' from the women.

'Wish I could come with you!' Wilbur Middleton said hoarsely.

'You stay home and keep the ladies happy!' someone shouted.

More ribald laughter.

Matt, Joe and Sheriff Cole led the posse out of town due east. There were ten men in the group and they all jogged along in high spirits, some of them actually singing songs they had learned in the army during the Civil War. Matt had heard those songs before, and he had read the speeches of Abraham Lincoln and various books about the war. He knew that war was a bloody business. People joined the army and went out in high spirits to fight, but returned bloodied and weary and determined never to fight again. That was the way of the world.

As he rode along he remembered the look of amazement on the face of the bushwhacker they had shot in the draw. Nobody should die like that, he thought again, but that's the way life rolls along and we have to accept it as it is.

Before setting out he had shown Sheriff Cole the map. Cole had scrutinized it closely.

'So this is where the Shanklin spread is?' he asked.

'That's what Milo said.'

'This guy Milo, you think we can trust him?'

'I wouldn't trust him as far as I could throw him and I wouldn't rely on him to carry a message to the President himself,' Matt said, 'but I do know he was scared as hell of that Hammer character, who would have taken a shot at us at the Long Branch if that good bartender hadn't had the guts to level a shotgun at him.'

Cole nodded in agreement.

'How about the men in the posse?' Joe asked. 'Looks like they think they're out on some kind of spree. How many of them know how to use a gun?'

Cole chuckled. 'Oh, they all know how to use their guns, Mr Stowe. I don't think you need to worry on that score. Take old Jim here. He fought under that damned hell raiser Custer at one time. He'd shoot his own grandmother if necessary. So you don't need to worry about old Jim.'

Old Jim had a long grizzly beard and he looked as ancient as Methuselah. He sat as upright and stiff as a board in the saddle and was one of a few men in the posse not actually singing, since he was chewing tobacco and spitting tobacco juice into the passing sage as he rode along.

The Shanklin spread lay some two days' ride away. In the afternoon they looked for a suitable place to set up camp. By this time the men had sobered up considerably. Sheriff Cole sent out a detail to gather dead branches and brushwood for the fire and Joe and several of the others started a cook-up. One of the younger men produced a harmonica and suggested a sing-song. Several of the men agreed, but the singing didn't last long. They were all tuckered out after the ride.

'I think we should get us as much sleep as we can,' Sheriff Cole said. 'We need to get ourselves fresh for tomorrow, you know. Can't afford to waste energy.'

So they built up the fire and kept it going in shifts through the night. They needed to: the temperature could drop quite dramatically in the early fall. The men spread their bedrolls as close as possible to the fire, but they would probably still shiver through the night.

Next morning the sun rose looking like a poached egg the cook had forgotten to scoop out of a cold pan. But Sheriff Cole and the brothers were already up, flapping their arms and stamping on the ground to shake the stiffness out of their limbs.

'Come and get it!' one of the cooks said from close to the fire.

The men piled in, took their feed and felt somewhat stronger.

Sheriff Cole and Matt pored over the map together.

'OK, boys, we hit the trail in ten minutes flat. So saddle up and get ready. Better check your hardware too, in case it lets you down when you need it.'

Some of the men seemed a little less enthusiastic than they had been the morning before and one man said,

'How do we know Abe Benjamin will be there when we arrive?'

'We can't know for certain,' Cole replied. 'We must hope we catch up with him sooner rather than later.'

They rode on throughout the day. Nobody was singing or playing the harmonica any more. The sun grew a little brighter and stronger, but a dark cloud looming on the horizon portended the first flurries of snow.

In the early afternoon, as they were riding among a small stand of cotton-woods, Sheriff Cole held up his arm and the party came to a standstill.

'There's a creek here,' Cole said. 'Time to give your horses a drink and fill your canteens and take a bite of jerky or pemmican, whatever you brought. According to the map the Shanklin place is no more than a mile or two from here.'

Old Jim, the man with the Methuselah beard, came into his own.

'Excuse me, Sheriff,' he said in a gruff tone. 'We can't just storm in there like a cavalry charge. They'll hear us coming long before we get there. I suggest two of these eager beavers go scouting ahead, see how the land lies.'

That sounded like good sense. Cole turned to the brothers.

'Why don't you two boys take a looksee and we'll keep under cover here until you report back.'

* * *

Matt and Joe rode to the head of the valley beyond which the Shanklin spread was reported to lie. They dismounted and tethered their mounts among the cottonwoods. Then they moved forward until they reached the rim. They looked down, hoping to see something of the Shanklin spread.

What they actually saw was somewhat disappointing. A ranch house of modest proportions with a wreath of smoke curling up from its stone chimney stood beside a corral with a several horses grazing peacefully. A few cattle were chewing the cud close by, and a line carried shirts and underpants flapping from it.

Matt took out his telescope and scanned slowly across the scene. It looked serene enough, he thought. Too serene, perhaps.

'You think Milo has fooled us?' Joe said quietly from beside him.

'I don't think so unless he's the best actor in the world,' Matt said, running his telescope along the ranch house for a better view. As he did so, the ranch house door opened and two women emerged. They both looked perfectly ordinary — homely, in fact. One held a basket while the other reached up and started to unpeg the shirts and underpants.

'Two women,' Matt said, handing the telescope to his brother. Joe peered at the women and gave a brief chuckle.

'They seem sort of domesticated,' he said. 'Like two women in a town somewhere.'

'Did you boys want something?' a voice came from behind them.

They spun round and found themselves looking down the barrel of two Colt forty-fives. Behind one of them was the ugly form of Hammer Macvey and behind the other was his buddy, who looked equally menacing.

'We were just taking a looksee,' Joe said with surprising calmness.

Hammer Macvey gave a somewhat unfriendly grin.

'Why don't you get yourselves up on your hind legs so you can see a whole lot better,' he suggested with a slight motion of his shooter.

The brothers rose cautiously.

'That's right,' Hammer said. 'Now keep your hands above your heads and get yourselves set to face your executioners.'

The brothers said nothing. They just got up and did as they were told. *We've been damned fools again*, Matt thought. *Just like two amateurs alone in the big wide forest!*

Hammer cocked his pistol and held it up straight close to his shoulder.

'I remember you two young cocks,' he said. 'You were in the Long Branch not so long ago and, unless I'm a Dutchman, it was you who gunned down on my buddy and killed him in Wolf Gully in recent days.'

'That was self-defence,' Joe said. 'He gunned down on us and killed my horse. So we had no choice. It was kill or be killed.'

Hammer gave a sharp guffaw of laughter.

'You've got a lot to say for yourself,

sonny. Speaking of kill or be killed, that might be your last speech on earth. Had you thought about that?'

He sidled up to Joe and tapped him on the chest with the barrel of his Colt. Joe drew back a pace and Matt seized his chance. He moved in quickly and pushed Hammer's Colt away from his brother's chest. It was a crazy move and Hammer pulled the trigger.

There was a loud explosion. Joe reeled back and fell to the ground. Now Matt became a wild beast. He grabbed Hammer's gun hand and thrust his head right into the man's pockmarked face. Hammer was a big and strong man, but the force of Matt's head-butt against his nose threw him off balance. He staggered away, snorting out blood. Hammer's buddy lumbered forward, but Matt was so close to Hammer that he couldn't get a shot in.

Joe rolled away, drew his Colt Frontier and fired at Hammer's buddy. It was a quick, impulsive shot and it caught the man high in the leg. The man screamed and went down like a felled pine tree.

Matt drew his Colt Frontier and cocked it.

Hammer was staggering like a blind man, but a blind man with a gun is no laughing matter. He had fired two shots in Matt's direction before Matt brought his gun into play. Matt fired just one shot. The bullet hit Hammer like a blast from hell. He leaped away and landed flat on his back. But still he wasn't finished. He tried to bring his gun round but it was just a second too late.

As Matt leaned over him he stared at Matt in astonishment, then gasped, shuddered and died.

Joe was lying on his back with blood pouring from his chest. Hammer's buddy was on his side, clutching his wounded leg. Matt took the man's gun and kicked it away.

'One more move from you and you're a dead man,' he shouted.

The man howled in agony.

Matt got down close to his brother to

examine his wound, which was high on the shoulder and bleeding profusely. It looked as though the bones had been smashed.

'Keep yourself still,' Matt said. 'We've got to stop the bleeding and bind you up.'

'Did I get him?' Joe growled.

'You got him,' Matt assured him. 'You got him good.'

Matt tore off Hammer's shirt and ripped it up to make some sort of bandage. It wasn't much of a bandage, especially from an *hombre* as poisonous as Hammer, but it would have to do. Matt was so intent on the job that he hardly noticed when Sheriff Cole and the posse rode up.

9

Cole looked down on the scene through grim grey eyes.

'So one man dead and two men wounded,' he said. We heard the shooting and came galloping. Who's this big galoot?'

'That's Hammer Macvey,' Matt said. He was too busy working on Joe's shoulder to take much interest in the question.

The other members of the posse were staring down at the battle scene in amazement. All except old Jim, who dismounted and came close to look at Joe.

'Busted shoulder,' he pronounced. 'Seen a lot of them in the war.'

He took down his saddle-bag and started rooting around inside it. Then he knelt down beside Matt and inspected Joe's wound.

'Looks like the slug might still be in there somewhere. We have to get it out clean and fast to save the patient.'

'Are you a doctor?' Joe asked him.

The old man grinned. 'I'm the nearest thing you're gonna get out here,' he said.

The man with the wound in the leg cried out, 'I got a bullet in the leg. Can't someone help me?'

Old Jim turned to look at him. 'You'll get all the help we can give you after we've fixed our good friend here.'

Sheriff Cole dismounted and started to inspect the man's wound.

'The bullet passed clean through,' he said after a minute. 'Looks like he'll survive.'

'You got some of that whiskey you carry?' old Jim asked. 'Clean out the wound as much as you can and give it a good measure of whiskey. That should do the job.'

Joe stared up at his brother through pain-glazed eyes.

'Am I dying?' he asked.

'You ain't dying, boy,' the old soldier said. 'If you were dying you wouldn't be talking like this. I'm gonna give you a good shot of whiskey and get that slug out of you before it turns bad.'

They gave Joe what seemed like a half-gallon of whiskey and stuck a hickory stick between his teeth so he could bite hard against it. Then the old man got to work on his shoulder with a Bowie knife, which he heated on a fire they had built. Joe gritted his teeth against the hickory stick and almost bit it in two before he passed out.

Old Jim was no slouch with that Bowie knife. He worked with confidence until he managed to probe the bullet out of Joe's shoulder.

'Can't speak for the shoulder or the ribs but at least the lungs seem to be OK,' he pronounced. 'Now we cover him with blankets and keep him warm.'

Joe spat out the hickory stick and groaned.

'You keep still, you're going to live,' Matt told him. 'Think of that girl Bethany you aim to marry. Now try to sleep.'

'Moisten his lips with water,' the old man said. 'Then maybe he'll sleep.'

Cole was looking down on the scene through grim eyes. He looked at the gunman.

'What are you howling for? You're alive ain't you? The bullet passed through your leg muscle but it didn't break a bone. So if you're lucky you'll live long enough to hang. You might have a stiff leg but you'll still be able to ride, if you can hoist yourself into the saddle.'

They had found the bullet that had passed through the man's leg on the ground close by. It had gone through clean as a whistle.

'Now, I think I need to ask you a few questions,' the sheriff said to him.

'I don't know a thing. I'm just a simple cowpuncher.'

Cole gave a grunt. 'A simple cowpuncher with a gun.'

'That's for protection.'

'Well, now, maybe you should tell us your name, simple cowpuncher with a gun.'

The man paused for a moment. 'Name's Billings.'

'Billings what?'

'They call me Cal.'

'Cal Billings.' Cole pondered for a moment. 'Who do you work for, Billiings?'

Billings grimaced and pressed his hand to his leg.

'This leg hurts bad and I'm as thirsty as hell. Give me something to drink.'

Cole motioned with his head and a member of the posse gave Billings a drink from his canteen.

'You know, Billings, we could string you up right here if we could find a good tree. Are you aware of that?'

Billings gritted his teeth. 'You wouldn't do that, Sheriff. Not if you have any respect for the law.'

Matt was looking down at the ranch house. Now there was no sign of life, but he knew there must be people down there: the two women he had seen earlier and probably some men too.

'You work for Shanklin?' he asked Billings.

'Have been,' Billings admitted.

'What about Abe Benjamin?' Sheriff Cole asked.

For a moment Billings said nothing. Then he saw Cole looking at his leg.

'Yeah, I know Benjamin,' he admitted.

'Then you must know he has a price on his head for robbing banks?'

Billings shook his head and stayed silent.

Sheriff Cole said: 'You're a damned fool, Billings, if you don't realize you're in this right up to your dainty little ears.'

That caused a hearty guffaw from the rest of the posse, since Billings's ears were quite pronounced and as red as the stripes on the Union flag.

'It might be of considerable benefit to you if you told us all you know. You might even get a medal of some sort.'

'Yeah, a tin medal with the devil's head on it,' one of the posse said.

There was another guffaw.

'Listen, Sheriff,' Matt said. 'I want

Benjamin as much as you do, but I'm worried about my brother. I'm going to ride down to that ranch house and get myself a wagon of some sort if they've got one. Joe needs peace and quiet and time to heal and he's not about to get it on the open prairie.'

Cole nodded. 'That sounds reasonable. Why don't we ride down right now? Old Jim can look after the patients, and me and some of the boys will ride with you down to the ranch house.'

So Sheriff Cole and Matt and three of the posse rode down to the ranch house, which seemed like a little paradise of peace. Nevertheless, they spread out and approached cautiously, Matt studying the set-up. In the corral there were just a few horses grazing, but a big dog started barking and howling as they approached.

'We might have to shoot that critter,' the sheriff said, 'before he scares hell out of the horses.'

Matt continued to study the surroundings. There was a windmill, a pool substantial enough to supply the ranch with water, and a drinking trough for the livestock. He saw hoofmarks in abundance, but no cattle. He got down from his horse and prodded a cowpat with his heel.

'There was a whole herd grazing here no more than two days back,' he said. 'Looks like they've been herded on to Ellsworth or Abilene. Mostly rustled, I guess. Should be as easy as picking blueberries to track.'

'As long as you remember some kind of berries sting,' Cole rejoined.

Now the door of the ranch house swung open and the two women Matt had seen at the washing-line came out on to the stoop. The big brown dog rushed forward to bark and snarl at the riders and the horses started to prick their ears and skitter.

The two women shaded their eyes against the sun and looked up at the men.

'Did you gentlemen want something?' the older woman asked in a deepish tone. She was a fine-looking woman, well dressed and confident. The younger woman looked alert and shrewd. Neither of them seemed put out by the arrival of strangers.

'Are you Mrs Shanklin?' the sheriff enquired of the older woman.

She looked him over appraisingly.

'Who would be asking?' she said with an Irish lilt.

'I'm Sheriff Cole of Clintock town,' the sheriff informed her. 'Perhaps you'd be kind enough to call off that dog of yours before he throws himself into a fit.'

The younger woman hushed up the dog who, they gathered, was appropriately called Wolf. Then she spoke up.

'We heard shooting earlier.'

'Yes, ma'am.' Cole touched the brim of his Stetson. 'Two *hombres* gunned down on some of my men. Man called Hammer Macvey and the other called Billings.'

'Hammer?' said the supposed Mrs Shanklin.

'Yes, ma'am, Hammer,' Cole said. 'I'm afraid he's dead.'

The two women looked slightly startled.

'Dead?' said the older woman.

'He's on the last round-up,' Cole affirmed. 'And Billings got shot through the leg. I don't suppose you can lend us a buckboard or a wagon of some kind?'

Mrs Shanklin looked doubtful.

'My husband's away right now,' she said. 'Could be gone as much as a week or more.'

'Herding cattle?' Cole speculated.

'Could be,' she agreed.

'Well then, Mrs Shanklin, the question is can you lend us a wagon? We've got a wounded man and he needs rest. We can't expect him to ride.'

The two woman exchanged glances and seemed uncertain.

'I guess we could help, that is if you're riding back to Clintock. If not, why doesn't he rest up here in the ranch house until he's strong enough to ride?'

Cole tipped his hat again. 'Well, that's very kind of you, ma'am. The trouble is we need to ride on as soon as maybe. If we could hire that wagon of yours some of us could take our man back to Clintock while the others ride on.'

There was another pause. Matt could see the two women were stalling for time.

'Ride on to where?' the older woman asked.

Cole was smiling quite benignly, a somewhat deceptive smile.

'We have an appointment with a man call Abe Benjamin,' he said. 'D'you happen to know him?'

'We don't know Benjamin,' the younger woman said abruptly but not altogether convincingly. 'We don't know the names of all my father's hands. He employs them on a seasonal basis.'

'Well, I guess you'd know Benjamin, on account of he and his buddies rob banks.'

'Is that so?' Mrs Shanklin laughed.

'That is surely so. He and his gang robbed a bank in Clintock recently and before that he robbed a bank in Dodge

City. There's a price on his head.'

'A price on the head of Abe Benjamin?' Mrs Shanklin said.

'So you do know him, Mrs Shanklin?'

Mrs Shanklin flushed up but still looked belligerent.

'Did you say your man is herding cattle to Ellsworth?' Cole asked.

'Could be,' Mrs Shanklin said. 'We don't know about the business. We just keep house and look after the property. Like I said, he'll probably be away for a few days.'

Cole said, 'Thank you, ma'am,' and tipped his hat again, somewhat ironically.

'Mind if I look in the barn and the tack room, ma'am?' Matt asked equally politely.

'Why would you want to do that?' the woman asked. 'There's just saddles and hay in there, and maybe a few rats.'

Matt said: 'All the same I'd like to take a looksee.'

Mrs Shanklin cocked her head towards the younger woman.

'Joanna, show this boy the barn, will you? And make sure he doesn't eat too much hay.'

The members of the posse guffawed at Matt's expense. He grinned at the younger woman. She tossed her head without saying anything. Matt dismounted and followed her beyond the ranch house and on towards the barn, which was divided rather neatly into a hay storage area and a tack room. As she walked the woman called Joanna held her head high and moved her hips, not too obviously but enough to attract Matt's attention.

'You want to tell me what you're looking for?' she asked suggestively when they reached the tack room.

'Branding-irons,' he said. 'What's the name of your brand?'

'We're the Bar Eight,' she said without hesitation.

When he went inside he had to pass close to her. She leaned towards him slightly.

'Is that all you want?' she murmured.

He went into the tack room, then turned. Everything smelled of leather and iron and a faint woman's scent. She stood before him with her head pushed slightly forward.

'You want to taste my lips?' he heard her say, so quietly that he thought he might have imagined it. He could hear the men of the posse talking and laughing with Mrs Shanklin outside.

He paused for no more than a second.

'Right now,' he managed to say, 'I have only two things on my mind: my wounded brother and that branding-iron I spoke of.'

The woman laughed quietly. It was a faint but musical laugh.

'I'm making you an offer you can't refuse,' she whispered.

It was as though a witch had cast a spell over him. For a moment he felt himself weakening. But then he shook his head clear.

'I've got to look at that branding-iron,' he said.

When he turned he could see the

irons in a stack against the wall. He picked out one and held it up. It was the Bar Eight. He examined it closely and saw in his mind that it could easily be used to obliterate the snake of Calloway's Snake outfit.

'This is interesting,' he said.

'More interesting than me?' she asked. But the spell was broken.

'Maybe some other time,' he said. 'Right now, I'll take possession of this branding-iron.' As he went out through the door he could feel her behind him and knew she was tempted to bring another branding-iron down on his head.

★   ★   ★

They took possession of the wagon and drove it back to where Joe lay. Old Jim had cared for him well but Joe complained bitterly.

'I'll be OK,' he said. 'I can ride and I can shoot. I want to ride on and nail those skookums, just like you.'

'I don't think so,' old Jim told him.

'We got to get you back to Clintock. The doc there knows what he's doing and you don't want to lose that arm, do you?'

Joe was already running a fever and Matt was worried about him. The plan was that old Jim would take care of him on the journey with two of the other members of the posse, while the rest of the posse rode on in pursuit of the rustlers.

Mrs Shanklin had become remarkably compliant, like her daughter.

'You can borrow that wagon,' she had said, 'just as long as you bring it back in one piece and in good order.'

Sheriff Cole had promised they'd do their best.

Following the cattle trail away from the ranch was a cinch. There must have been at least 200 head of cattle and a chuck wagon. Cole's posse was now cut down to six men: Cole, Matt, and four others, including the harmonica player and Luke Hamplin who always sounded optimistic.

As they left the ranch, Matt was

examining the tracks. Something caught his eye. He dismounted and examined the tracks more closely.

'Look at these tracks,' he said to Cole, 'and look at these horse-droppings.'

Cole squinted at the trail and saw what Matt referred to: fresh tracks and horse dung quite separate from the main herd.

'You know what this means, Sheriff?' Matt said.

'I know right well what it means,' Cole replied. 'It means that when those two women were sweet-talking us, one of the hands who had stayed behind on the ranch for some reason rode off to give warning to Shanklin and Abe Benjamin.'

'Which means,' said Luke Hamplin, 'they'll be expecting us and waiting for us.'

A veil of silence fell over the group.

'They'll be waiting and ready for us,' the harmonica player, Pete, agreed.

Cole nodded to Matt and turned in his saddle.

'Well, boys, it's like this: there's no way we can surprise Shanklin and his bunch. Abe Benjamin will be looking for somewhere he can shoot down at us from cover. If we're not careful we'll be like ducks in a shooting gallery.'

'What are we gonna do?' Pete asked, somewhat less confidently.

'Well, boys, I mean to go on, but you have to make up your own minds. If you want to go back I'm not gonna blame you. You go back with a clean sheet and nobody will think less of you.' He was looking at Matt again. Matt stirred himself.

'I'm with you all the way, Sheriff. It's time Abe Benjamin and his bunch cashed in their chips.'

That went some way to giving heart to the others.

'Sure is,' Luke Hamplin said. 'So, I'm with you too, Sheriff.'

'If we yellowed-out on you now, we'd be letting down our friend Joe, wouldn't we?' Pete added. 'If he goes down we'd be no more than rats leaving a sinking ship.'

Jeremiah Hopkins and Giles agreed.

'We have to use tactics here,' the sheriff said. 'It's no use just riding along the trail like a bunch of geese following a dozy farm hand. That way we'd be cooking in the pot come sundown.'

'I thought you said ducks,' Luke Hamplin said with a laugh.

'Fish or fowl, it makes no never mind,' Pete added.

The only one who didn't give his opinion was Jeremiah Hopkins, a somewhat taciturn individual who occasionally rode shotgun on the stage between Clintock and Dodge City.

Matt said: 'Someone should scout ahead while we keep to the higher ground away from the trail.'

'That's agreed,' Cole said. 'And another thing: we don't know how far ahead the herd is. Could be more than a day. Cattle move slowly. You don't want to push them too hard. Twenty miles a day is enough. I guess they'll be no more than two days ahead, maybe less. That's about forty miles at the most. I figure it's three or four days' ride to Ellsworth. We should catch up on them by tomorrow at sundown.'

'That means we roost tonight in a cold camp,' Matt said. 'If we light a fire Abe Benjamin could come down on us like the hordes on Nineveh.'

'Who the hell would they be?' Luke Hamplin asked.

'Don't show your ignorance, boy,' Cole said. But he didn't attempt to throw any light on the subject.

Matt scouted ahead with Jeremiah Hopkins. Though Hopkins was a close-mouthed *hombre* he seemed staunch and reliable enough. And, like Matt, he was adept at reading the signs. If they spotted something or got into trouble he would ride back to warn the others.

'They're not too far ahead,' he told Matt, after examining the tracks. 'We could overtake them soon after sunup tomorrow. That's what I figure.'

Matt agreed. And so they rode on through the day without let or hindrance.

Before sundown they chose a camp-site in a reasonably sheltered place, a little off the trail to the right. Hopkins rode back to bring in the others. They hobbled their horses and dished out the cold food they had available. Then Cole addressed the men like President Lincoln giving his Gettysburg address.

'Now, men, this is a tough assignment. We have to maintain camp silence throughout the night. We don't want to attract attention from Abe Benjamin and his bunch. Remember, they know we're coming, but they don't know where we are and we have to keep it that way. So we must set up guard, one hour each through the night. I'll take the first watch . . . '

He told each of them when to take his turn. Most of the men didn't have timepieces, so through the night they had to rely on those who had.

Matt found it difficult to sleep. He kept thinking of Joe, his younger brother, and of how he might die from complications. His mind also switched back to the wonderful young woman, Bell Inkpen, who would be waiting for him at the Inkpen ranch. When a man sleeps fitfully, he dreams wild dreams and Matt also dreamed of the woman offering herself to him at the Shanklin ranch. In his dream she whispered lustful thoughts and leaned towards him with her dress stripped away and her pale breasts revealed invitingly.

Suddenly he woke with a start and grabbed for his gun. Something or someone was stirring in the undergrowth, maybe creeping up on them. He rolled out of his bedroll and cocked his gun. Luke Hamplin, who was supposed to be on guard, was dead to the world, his head hanging down, his gun between his legs, his back to a cottonwood tree. He was snoring none too melodiously. Light was filtering through the cottonwoods, so Matt knew it was close to sunup.

He stood up beside a tree and peered around cautiously. Possibly the horses had woken him, or maybe a coyote had come browsing close to the camp, or possibly a grizzly bear. *Don't get jittery,* he thought. *Keep yourself calm.*

Luke Hamplin opened his eyes and shook his head.

'You hear something?' he asked.

Matt didn't bother to tell him he'd been asleep on guard. There wasn't time to say anything because Sheriff Cole was already on his feet.

'Time to move on,' the sheriff said. 'Get your breakfast, boys, check your guns and your horses, then we'll move out.'

But before they could saddle up they heard the sound of horses approaching. Six riders came riding through the cottonwoods. Matt drew his Colt but Cole and the others were just a moment too late. Abe Benjamin and his bunch had guns trained on them and Benjamin was laughing. Matt saw despite the half light that Benjamin was riding Joe's horse, Sentinel.

'You boys riding trail hand?' Benjamin called out. He sounded almost friendly but Matt saw that the Remington was pointed straight at him.

'I believe you must be Abe Benjamin,' Cole said calmly.

'Who wants to know?' Benjamin asked.

'Sheriff Cole of Clintock wants to know,' Cole said.

'My, my, we have a sheriff here,' Benjamin joked. 'And why would you want to know that, Mr Cole?'

'On account of you're wanted for robbing the Clintock bank.' Cole sounded remarkably composed, as though he himself held the gun.

Matt was looking at Benjamin's companions but there was no one he recognized. They were all levelling their weapons at members of the posse and looked ready to use them at any time Benjamin gave the order.

I've been a damned clumsy fool again, Matt thought.

Benjamin was still looking at him through eyes that glittered with malice.

'You're the boy who killed that bully Shamanzo,' he said. 'I remember you well. You deserve a medal for that. What are you doing out here, boy?'

Keep talking, Matt thought to himself. Make the man laugh.

'I'm tracking skunks,' he said with a false smile.

'Skunks, is it?' Benjamin said. 'What kind of skunks would they be?'

'The worst kind,' Matt said. 'The kind that steal other men's horses and rob banks.'

Benjamin started to laugh and, as he laughed, his gun wavered. Matt acted impulsively. He dropped down on his knees, aimed his Colt Frontier and fired. Sentinel reared up and Benjamin fell back.

Then all hell broke loose. The horses pranced and reared and Benjamin's henchmen started to fire at the posse members. Taking aim from a prancing horse is more a matter of chance than accuracy but a man on the ground has an advantage if he stays cool and calm.

Sheriff Cole was such a man. He moved as calmly as a predatory animal, firing and moving and kneeling and firing again. He didn't just rely on instinct; he held his gun out straight, took careful aim, and fired just like the gunfighter Wyatt Earp.

Matt saw two men go down before the rest of the bunch wheeled away and tried to retreat. But the action wasn't all on one side. The optimist, Luke Hamplin, had been thrown back by a bullet and he lay still, with his gun pointing at the sky. And Jeremiah Hopkins lay moaning and crying with his hand pressed to his chest.

Sentinel was still rearing and whinnying. Matt ran forward to grab the reins and calm him.

Sheriff Cole lurched forward just as Abe Benjamin half-rose from the ground and fired a shot. Cole jerked back, then rolled over and lay still. Now Benjamin was on his knees, cocking his Remington. Matt ran in and kicked at the Remington, which exploded harmlessly in the air. Matt was taking no chances. He stamped down hard on Abe Benjamin and kicked him twice in the ribs. Benjamin covered his face with his hands and lay quivering. Matt kicked his gun away and went to Sheriff Cole.

Cole lay gasping on his back. 'What happened?' he asked. 'I can't see a damned thing.'

Matt knelt beside him. 'Where are you hit?' he asked.

'I'm killed,' the sheriff said. 'I'm blind.' He lay gasping for a second, then quivered all over and died.

*　　*　　*

It had been a costly victory. The sheriff was dead; Luke Hamplin would laugh no more; and Jeremiah Hopkins was severely wounded in the chest. That left Matt, Pete the harmonica player and the man called Giles. On the other side, two of Benjamin's henchmen were dead, picked off by Sheriff Cole's withering fire before he himself fell. But, though bruised and battered and wounded, Benjamin was alive. Four men were dead and one was possibly dying.

Pete was in a state of severe shock.

'What do we do now?' he asked hopelessly.

Matt knew he had to take charge. 'What we do is, we take these men back to Clintock,' he said.

'Cole was my best friend,' the harmonica player moaned.

'He was a good man,' Matt agreed.

10

They hoisted the bodies of Luke Hamplin and Sheriff Cole on to the backs of their horses. Although it was crude and undignified it was the only thing they could do. They patched up Jeremiah Hopkins and somehow got him on to his horse too. Hopkins didn't complain; he wasn't a complaining kind of man.

'Am I gonna live?' he asked Matt.

'I believe you will,' Matt assured him, though he wasn't as hopeful as he sounded. The wound was high in the chest and it was impossible to say how deeply the bullet was lodged. Hopkins leaned forward in the saddle and gritted his teeth.

Abe Benjamin was in better shape than Matt had expected. He was wounded and battered but he would survive long enough to get him to trial.

'Don't tie my hands, boy,' he pleaded with Matt. 'You truss me up like a chicken ready for the oven I might just as well be stiff and dead.'

Matt didn't tie his hands. He just looped a rope round his waist so that, if he tried to escape, he could yank him off his horse. Matt would ride behind him and keep an eye on him all the way back to Clintock. It would be a hard ride and they would need to spend one night at least in the open, which would endanger the life of Jeremiah Hopkins even more.

Another thing that worried Matt was some of the Benjamin bunch might want to bushwhack what remained of the posse and free Abe Benjamin.

He said to Benjamin, 'If any of your boys try to jump us and free you, they're going to be disappointed because the first thing I'm going to do is shoot you dead, you hear me?' Matt spoke without emotion and without any particular feeling at all.

'I understand you, boy,' Benjamin

replied sombrely. Though he still referred to Matt as boy, he spoke to him with increasing respect. After all, hadn't Matt killed Shamanzo and Hammer? He might be only just twenty-two, the same age as Billy the Kid when he died, but Billy had killed one man for each of those twenty-two years, or so the legend said.

'You gonna turn me in, boy?' Benjamin asked Matt.

'Don't have much choice, do I?' Matt said. 'A man reaps what he sows and you've sowed a heap of bad seed in your time.'

'Not to mention the price on my head,' Benjamin said ironically.

Matt shook his head. 'Sure, the money figures, but the dead and the injured are a lot more important. They can't speak for themselves, so I have to speak for them.'

They were riding close but not close enough for Abe Benjamin to play any monkey tricks.

'You remember that time we came on you when you and your brother were cleaning up in the river?' Benjamin asked him.

'I remember it well, Abe.'

'You might also remember we took your horses and your money, but we left you Shamanzo's flea-bitten nag and your guns. We didn't take your guns, did we?'

Matt had to admit he was right.

'You might remember something else too,' Abe said. 'At that time I made a suggestion that you should ride with us. You remember that?'

'I remember it,' Matt replied, tight-lipped.

'It would have been a good deal, boy, but you chose different. You know why I made that offer?'

'I think I have some idea.'

'That was because I saw promise in you, boy. I knew you had the makings of a fine man. And I believe that's what you're becoming, boy.'

Matt wondered where all this was leading, though he had a shrewd suspicion.

Abe Benjamin nodded slowly. 'I'm

lucky I didn't die back there,' he said. 'You could have killed me after I shot the sheriff, but you just kicked me around a little.'

'That's true,' Matt admitted. 'And I have to agree I was strongly tempted to kill you. You'd have killed the whole bunch of us if you could.'

'Well, it's dog eat dog out here,' Benjamin said. 'Kill or be killed. So I'm going to put it to you: you help me to escape I'll give you a thousand dollars. How does that smell to you?'

'I don't rightly know,' Matt said. 'I haven't seen the colour of your money, but I think it stinks like rancid meat, Mr Benjamin.'

'That sounds like a quotation from some big writer,' Benjamin said with a laugh.

'Well, it isn't in the Bible,' Matt said.

⋆　⋆　⋆

Come sundown they were making reasonable progress towards Clintock.

Matt would have pressed on but he thought it wise to stop for the night, and Jeremiah Hopkins was starting to keen and moan to himself. They found a good place in a cave overlooking what passed for a trail, where nobody could creep up on them unawares, and then they settled down for the night. They even lit a fire and risked being seen. As the dusk came creeping in they heard the sound of coyotes yapping and howling in the hills near by. It was an ugly sound but not as sinister as the howl of wolves. They took the corpses down from their horses and laid them on the ground with blankets over their faces, not too close to the fire.

'We should have left them where they lay,' Pete complained. 'We could have heaped rocks on them to keep the coyotes away.'

Matt didn't agree. 'They were good men and we need to show them respect,' he said.

After the meal, which although frugal was exceedingly welcome, Matt decided they should take watch, hour on hour. Since there were only three of them that meant a long stint each. But with the first streaks of dawn they would ride on. After Abe Benjamin had eaten his fill and relieved himself outside the cave, Matt tied his wrists and attached the rope to a stake which he drove into the ground.

'Sleep easy,' he said. 'And remember what I said. If any of your *amigos* try to rescue you in the night I'm going to shoot you right through the head.'

'I think I believe you,' Benjamin said with a grin. 'Like I said, you're growing into a man. And maybe you'll consider my offer, too.'

Matt made no reply. He could hear Jeremiah Hopkins moaning and swearing quietly to himself.

'I think I'm going,' Hopkins said to him. 'You think you can help me? Give me a drop of water to drink?'

Matt helped him to sit up and gulp down a drop of water from his canteen.

'You know how to pray?' Hopkins asked.

Matt had never thought much about

prayer. His mother had taught him the Lord's Prayer and one or two other scraps but he hadn't said much in the way of prayer since he was a kid. But when a dying man asks you to pray with him you have to come up with something, so he started improvising prayers.

Hopkins said 'amen' occasionally. Then he coughed and choked and died.

Matt covered his face with a blanket and crawled over to his own sleeping-place. Suddenly he didn't feel in the least sleepy. His pulse was racing hard and he felt like rushing out among the cottonwoods, shouting and screaming defiance.

He was still awake when the first rays of dawn came slanting through the trees.

'OK,' he said to Pete and Giles. 'Now we ride on. We should hit Clintock by early afternoon by my reckoning.'

★ ★ ★

Matt's calculations were right and the sad procession rode into Clintock shortly after midday. Three living members of the posse, three dead men hanging across their horses, and one prisoner. The people of Clintock had been expecting them. The day before, the other sad procession had come in with the Shanklin wagon.

A great wail went up from the people when they saw the bodies of the sheriff, Luke Hamplin, and Jeremiah Hopkins. Among them were Meg Cole and her daughter, Charlotte and Wilbur Middleton, their friends, and Mrs Jeremiah Hopkins, who screamed when she saw her dead husband. The town funeral director was also on the scene.

'We must get these men down from their horses,' he declared. 'This is no way to treat a dead man.'

The corpses were brought down with great respect and everyone clamoured to know about the catastrophe and how they had been killed. Some even wanted to lynch Abe Benjamin on the spot, but Matt stepped in.

'He must lodge in the jailhouse and

wait for his trial,' he insisted. The only person who had the key to the jail was Meg Cole, the sheriff's widow. So Matt took charge.

When Benjamin was safely behind bars he gave Matt a wry grin.

'Well, at least you saved my neck for another day,' he said.

Matt made no reply. He was thinking of his brother Joe.

'Joe's doing as well as can be expected,' old Jim told him. 'I looked after him as well as I could. He's at the hospital, being treated by the doc.'

Matt went to the hospital immediately to see his brother. Joe was sitting on a chair in the small ward with his arm in a sling and bandages across his chest. Doctor Francis had done his best and, although Joe had run a high fever, he was now a good deal better. When Joe saw Matt he brightened up considerably.

'Why, you look a complete mess!' he exclaimed.

'Well, I'm alive,' Matt said. For the

first time he saw himself as Joe saw him: he had a growth of heavy stubble and he wasn't exactly well-washed. He knew he probably stank, but no worse than those poor corpses lying in the funeral parlour.

'Well, at least you got Abe Benjamin,' Joe said. 'What about the rest of the bunch and Ned Shanklin?'

'Shanklin's for another day,' Matt said. 'At least we got a branding iron to show our friend Mr Calloway.'

*　*　*

Matt was on his way to the telegraph station when he met Wilbur Middleton.

'Well now, boy,' the old man said, stretching out his arms, 'this is indeed a very sad day, but we've got a lot to thank you for. My good wife wants you to come right back to the place and stay as long as you like. You can eat and take a hot bath and just lie back and relax, and you deserve it, young man.'

Matt didn't think he deserved much

at all, but he knew he would be in line for the reward for bringing in Abe Benjamin, and alive too.

'Thank you. I'll be glad to accept that generous offer,' he said.

Then he continued on his way down to the telegraph station and sent a message through to Sheriff Luke Potter, telling him what had happened and asking him to send a message to May Inkpen and the girls to tell them he and Joe were safe and would be returning just as soon as they could.

This was no easy matter. Matt still had Abe Benjamin in the prison and nobody would be entrusted with the key. And Joe was still not fit to ride, though when he heard that Sentinel was back and in good shape he was delighted.

Charlotte had made a huge tasty meal, but before Matt could indulge he sank deep into the bath, rested his head on the back, and thought. At least he thought he was thinking. When he woke with a start, the water had started to cool and Charlotte Middleton was framed in the door.

'Are you about to get your rump out of there, young man? Your dinner is ready in the pot and I want to serve it up before it spoils.'

Matt got himself out of the big, deep bath and towelled himself down. For a hick town this was highly civilized, he thought.

When he got to the table Wilbur Middleton and Charlotte were waiting for him. To his surprise Meg Cole and her daughter Ruby were there too.

'We invited Meg and Ruby so you can tell them what happened,' Charlotte explained.

Wilbur said a grace that was longer than usual because he added a bit about 'our dear friend and sheriff' and 'the men who had given their lives'.

As they ate their food Matt told the whole story, including the bravery of the men who had died, especially Sheriff Cole. As he spoke Meg Cole sat as stern as a post and, though Ruby looked as though she were on the point of tears, she managed to retain her composure. Matt noticed that neither of the women ate much.

After the meal it was time to sleep. Matt took his boots off and fell back on the bed. Almost as soon as his head touched the pillow he was dead to the world.

When he woke he knew he had made up his mind. The words 'old Jim' sprang up to confront him. Charlotte Middleton had prepared another of her generous breakfasts and he fell to with an appetite to match it.

'I've had a meal taken into the hospital for your brother. You're both heroes and you deserve it.'

'What about the prisoner?' Matt asked.

'Oh, he'll be fed,' she crowed. 'It's feed or hang. If a man's alive we feed him. If he's dead we don't need to because he's food for the crows.' She gave her high shrill laugh.

'Where's old Jim?' Matt asked her.

'Oh, he's around. You'll probably find him in the store, comforting Meg. He was a particular friend to the Coles.'

Like she said, old Jim was in the store commiserating with Mrs Cole. Jim didn't say much; he was the kind of man who comforted just by being there.

'I need to speak with you, Jim,' Matt said.

'Sure thing.'

They went outside and sat on a bench under the *ramada*.

'I have unfinished business to attend to,' Matt said. 'I have to ride back to Dodge City and make arrangements and I also have things to do about the Snake outfit.'

'Sure,' the old-timer acknowledged.

'Clintock has no sheriff right now and I want to give you the key to the jail. You're an old soldier and you know the way things run. I want you to make sure that that ornery bastard Abe Benjamin doesn't break out. Make sure he's fed and properly cared for until I make arrangements to have him brought to justice. Can you do that?'

'That'll be an honour, Captain,' old Jim said without a trace of irony.

Matt went back to the hospital to consult the doctor and visit with his brother. First he saw the doctor. Doc Francis had been doctor in Clintock for some years. He had come West as a tourist. He'd stopped off at Clintock, fallen in love with a local girl and decided to stay. Said he couldn't stand the hustle and bustle of the East and, anyway, Westerners needed care just as much as Easterners, so why not stay? He had trained his wife up as a nurse and she had proved an apt pupil in more ways than one.

'Can I talk with you about my brother?' Matt asked the doctor.

'Ask away, young man.' Doc Francis had a brusque and official manner but a kind eye.

'Is he going to recover?' Matt asked him directly. The doctor nodded slowly and gave his opinion.

'I think he'll recover,' he said, 'just as

long as he takes care.' He stroked his goatee beard. 'But he needs to rest up. That bullet smashed his shoulder and broke two of his ribs. Fortunately his lung wasn't punctured, so he should be OK. Only thing is his arm won't be much use. Luckily it's the left arm. So he'll need to rely on his right arm for everything in future.'

Matt was relieved but saddened. 'When will he be fit to ride?' he asked.

The doctor wrinkled his brow. 'I wouldn't recommend any riding at the moment. In the best of all worlds, he should be here in my care for at least another month, maybe longer.'

'That takes us to winter,' Matt said.

'That would be about right,' the doc agreed.

When Matt went into the hospital he found Joe sitting on a chair. Mrs Francis was adjusting his sling.

'I wanna go back to the Inkpen place,' Joe complained.

'And you will,' Matt assured him.

Mrs Francis left them and Matt sat

down with his brother.

'I have to talk to you straight,' he said. He told Joe that he might have to stay in Clintock for four weeks or so until the doc was satisfied he was fit to travel.

'But that takes us into the winter snows,' Joe said.

'You're being well looked after,' Matt told him. 'These people think you're a hero. So you couldn't be in a better place.'

It was difficult persuading Joe but at last he had to agree.

* * *

Matt didn't go directly to Dodge City. A message came back from the Inkpen ranch by telegraph. May and the girls had received Matt's message and they were glad that everyone was OK, except that Bethany was worried about Joe and wanted to see him as soon as possible.

Matt sent a message by return: he was going to the Snake outfit and would drop in on them on the way back.

Next morning early he set out for the Snake outfit. He arrived there before nightfall. Busby, the ramrod was out with the hands bringing some of the stock closer to the ranch. There had been rumours of more rustling, a new man informed him.

'You want to see Mr Calloway, I'll ride up with you,' the man said.

'Don't bother yourself,' Matt said. 'Mr Calloway will be expecting me sometime anyway.'

He rode up to the somewhat elaborate ranch house and dismounted. He walked across the deck and rapped on the door. A young woman opened the door and stared out at him.

'What do you want?' she asked somewhat abruptly.

'I've come to see Mr Calloway,' Matt said. 'I think he's expecting me. Just tell him it's Matt Stowe. I think he'll understand.'

The girl closed the door and left him

standing on the deck. It was quite frosty out there but he didn't have to wait long. After a minute the door opened again and Calloway beckoned him in. He was smoking one of his customary fat cigars and he looked like a plutocrat.

Matt went into a big room with a huge roaring log fire. He blinked around but there was nobody else in the room, not even the maid, though he could hear the tinkle of laughter from further off in another room. He held out the branding-iron he had borrowed from the Ned Shanklin outfit.

'So you found the place?' Calloway said.

'We found it and I know where they trade your rustled cattle, Mr Calloway.'

Calloway looked impressed.

Matt held out an improved version of the map Milo had drawn. It showed the exact location of the Ned Shanklin outfit with the trail to Ellsworth dotted in.

'Several men died for that,' Matt said, 'and my brother Joe was badly wounded. I think we earned our thousand dollars.'

Calloway studied him through stern grey eyes.

'Did I say that?' he asked.

'That's what you said, Mr Calloway — a thousand greenbacks.'

Calloway was looking at Matt's gunbelt with the butt of the Colt Frontier in its holster.

'A thousand dollars is an awful lot of money,' he said sceptically.

'Not too much,' Matt said. 'I think we kept our side of the deal.'

Calloway considered for a moment longer. 'How about if I paid a little extra,' he said.

'What would that be for, Mr Calloway?'

Calloway nodded and took a leisurely puff at his cigar.

'Suppose I asked you to lead a bunch of men to clean out Shanklin before he does any more damage . . . not only for me but for the Cattlemen's Association?' he asked.

Matt grinned. 'I'm not a gunman, Mr Calloway, and I don't care for killing. You're asking me to be part of a range war. Is that what you want?'

'Think about it, Mr Stowe,' the rancher said. 'I'll get your money.'

He left Matt to enjoy the fire and mooch around the room. Calloway was a long time gone and Matt heard murmurs from the other room. When Calloway returned he had a thick envelope stuffed with dollar bills. He held it out to Matt with some reluctance.

'You want me to sign for it?' Matt asked.

'No,' the rancher said. 'I just want you to think about my offer.'

'I'm thinking,' Matt said. 'And I'll let you know my decision later on.'

'Is that a promise?'

'That's a promise.'

★ ★ ★

Matt rode off from the Calloway spread for several miles. He could, perhaps, have slept in the bunkhouse, but he wasn't keen to meet any of the hands. He just wanted to be alone with his horse. He built a fire and a small shelter, and during the night it rained, not hard but enough to saturate a man in the open. Then the rain stopped and a few flakes of snow came drifting down. Fortunately, Matt's shelter had been well constructed, so he was reasonably well protected. But it was turning cold, so he got up before the first rays of sunrise had come slanting through. He decided to skirt round Dodge City and ride straight for the Inkpen place.

As he drew close he saw the ranch house coming out of the haze. Smoke was spiralling up from the chimney, and it was like a picture in a dream. But it was a cold day and soon there would be snow on the ground.

He rode forward and the door opened to reveal May and the girls. They were smiling, though a little anxiously.

'Where's Joe?' Bethany asked. This was the moment Matt had dreaded.

'I had to leave him in Clintock,' he said. 'He got wounded in the shoulder, but he's going to be OK.'

'I want to see him,' Bethany said in a rush.

'Right now he's resting up,' Matt said. 'The doc wants him to stay in the hospital there for a while. But I guess I can take you in the buggy whenever you're free.'

'I shall be free tomorrow morning,' Bethany insisted.

Then Bell appeared and for Matt it was like the sun shining out of the house. She was smiling and he started smiling back at her.

'How are you?' he asked her.

'I'm well,' she said. She seemed slightly breathless. 'Let me put your horse in the barn.'

Matt dismounted and together they walked the horse to the barn. After they had lodged the horse with the other horses, they turned towards one another and their lips came together as naturally as though they were in the Garden of Eden.

'You smell of smoke and horses and leather,' she murmured.

'I'm sorry about that.'

'No, I like it. It's a good wholesome manly smell.' They kissed again more deeply.

'When will you marry me?' he asked.

'Just as soon as we can arrange it,' she replied.

May had built up the fire in the cabin so high that the whole place was warm and much more welcoming than Calloway's fire could ever have been.

'So, you're engaged to be married?' May said.

'That seems to be the case.' Matt was smiling. 'That's if you give your consent.'

'My man Steve would have been delighted,' she said. 'So I can't have any objection, can I?'

Now that it was official Matt would sleep in the house and the two girls would share a bed. Everything now fell into place, except for the question of the mortgage hanging over May's head.

'The banker and the surveyor have been again,' Bethany said. 'They want us out of here come springtime.'

May looked at Bethany reprovingly.

Matt shook his head. 'I don't think we need to worry about that,' he said. 'I have funds.' He smiled at Bell and she reached out to take his hand.

Come morning they got out the buggy and harnessed the horses. Matt and Bethany drove off to Clintock together. The weather looked promising, so they should be OK. If the weather turned sour they could stay with the Middletons and drive back later. Bethany insisted on going straight to the hospital to see Joe.

When she saw him she broke down in tears and ran her hands gently over his broken arm.

'Oh, you poor man!' she cried. 'I want to take you home and look after you right away.'

Doc Francis was impressed, and it was clear that the lovers wanted to go back to the Inkpen ranch together. He relented.

'Keep him wrapped up warm,' he insisted.

So they set out next morning and drove back to the Inkpen ranch.

★ ★ ★

Abe Benjamin came up for trial in the spring. He pleaded guilty to robbing banks but not guilty of any killings. He certainly knew how to speak up for himself and he even made the judge laugh once or twice. Matt bore witness to the fact that he had seen Benjamin shoot Sheriff Cole, but Benjamin insisted it was self-defence. The sheriff, who was a great man and a fine shot, had intended to kill him, so he had to defend himself, but he hadn't meant to kill the sheriff; he just wanted to parley with him, and it had all been a terrible mistake.

The judge accepted his plea and gave him a large fine and a year in prison. When he was sentenced Benjamin rose from his seat and said in a loud voice:

'You're a real gent, Mr Justice, a real gent,' which caused roars of laughter from some of the people and howls of anger from the rest. Old Jim shouted out,

'He should be hanged good and proper!' and Charlotte Middleton cried,

'He killed a good man. He should be strung up from the highest tree and left to rot.'

The judge brought his gavel down hard and shouted, 'The court will rise!'

Outside the court Matt was assailed by a number of the Clintock people. Wilbur Middleton, usually so placid, had turned quite puce.

'What can we do?' he shouted at Matt, as though Matt was somehow to blame.

'You should have shot him out of hand,' Charlotte said. 'That judge is a fool. He has no respect for the law.'

What did Matt feel? He felt quite sick.

* * *

They say every cloud has a silver lining and this one certainly had. Two weeks after the trial there was a double wedding. Joe and Bethany were to be married in the small chapel in Dodge City and Matt and Bell were to be married at the same time.

Joe's arm and shoulder had healed well but the arm was now withering and useless and he kept his hand in his pocket. Yet Bethany was proud to be his wife; his right arm was stronger than ever and he was keen to work on the farm. Even a man with one arm can work well if he has a mind to it.

Matt was, perhaps, more of a thinking man, though he had a reputation for being good with a gun. Bell hated guns but she had great respect for Matt's intellectual acumen.

On the morning of the wedding the sun was riding like a pale ghost looking through a veil of cloud. May, who had made herself a fine outfit to mark the occasion, stepped out of the chapel on the arm of old Jim, who looked almost as sprightly as a boy in his store suit.

'This is a good day, May,' he said with unaccustomed cheerfulness.

'Every day is a good day,' she said, 'But this day is special. I've got two good husbands for my girls and the future looks good as well.' She gazed up at the ghostlike sun and said. 'Steve would be pleased too. I know he liked those boys.'

The two couples were standing on the church step as a photographer fussed around them.

'When I get ready to duck down say cheese,' he told them.

They stood like zombies, stretched their lips and froze in time.

The fading sepia photograph hung on the wall of the Inkpen ranch for several generations. Nobody knows where it is now, but that doesn't matter. Time rolls on and people pass on with it, and that doesn't matter either. They have lived their lives and enjoyed most of their days.

The farm grew and the Stowes and the Inkpens grew with it, and so the clock ticks on.